THE SOLDIER'S
SWEETHEART

THE SOLDIER'S SWEETHEART

BY

SORAYA LANE

First published in Great Britain 2013
by Mills & Boon, an imprint of Harlequin (UK) Limited.
Large Print edition 2013
Harlequin (UK) Limited, Eton House,
18-24 Paradise Road, Richmond, Surrey TW9 1SR

© Harlequin Books S.A. 2013

Special thanks and acknowledgement are given to
Soraya Lane for her contribution to THE LARKVILLE
LEGACY series.

ISBN: 978 0 263 23672 9

Harlequin (UK) policy is to use papers that are natural,
renewable and recyclable products and made from
wood grown in sustainable forests. The logging and
manufacturing process conform to the legal environmental
regulations of the country of origin.

Printed and bound in Great Britain
by CPI Antony Rowe, Chippenham, Wiltshire

For Natalie & Nicola.
Thank you so much for your encouragement,
support and friendship.
I don't know what I'd do without
our daily email chats!

CHAPTER ONE

NATE CALHOUN held up one hand to shield his face from the sun. He'd forgotten what it was like to look out over the land, to see grass stretching so far into the distance that he couldn't tell where their ranch ended and the next one began.

Sand he was used to, but not grass.

He pulled the door shut behind him and stretched out his right leg, trying not to grimace. His damn calf wouldn't stop throbbing, and no matter how much he tried to ignore it, walking wasn't as easy as it used to be.

Nate glanced up at the main house, knew exactly what he'd find if he walked over. Nancy, their long-time housekeeper, would be clearing the breakfast dishes; there'd still be the smell of strong coffee lingering in the air, and there'd probably be some leftovers waiting to be eaten. But he wasn't ready to be part of that life again, didn't know when he'd be able to answer the questions his family seemed so intent on asking him whenever he spent time with them.

It was why he'd walked away from them all on his first night back and taken over the unused guesthouse.

Nate turned and walked a track that was still oddly familiar to him. As a boy, right up until he'd left the ranch to join the army, he'd wandered to a massive tree tucked far enough away from the house to be private. Where a weathered timber swing had tilted back and forth in the breeze. Somewhere that he'd never shared with anyone except for…

Who the hell was that?

Nate stopped and squinted. He was close enough to see the tree but not close enough to figure out who was sitting on a swing that he'd expected to be long gone by now.

He straightened and tried his hardest not to

limp, even though he knew that disguising his injury was impossible.

Then the mystery figure on the swing turned his way.

Nate gulped. Hard. Before grinding his teeth together and walking toward her.

It was Sarah. After all these years, he'd managed to find Sarah Anderson under his tree.

Some things would never change.

She stood as he approached, a shy smile making her lips tilt ever so slightly in the corners, a faint blush creeping across her cheeks.

"Hey, Nate."

He did his best to return the smile, but the truth was that simple things like grinning at a friend didn't come so easy to him anymore. And besides, he didn't even know if he could call Sarah a friend these days, not after what had happened between them.

"Sarah," he managed, stopping a few paces from her.

She hesitated, flushed all over again, before

leaning awkwardly into him and giving him a hug.

Nate stiffened, tried to relax and found it impossible. Even with Sarah's gentle embrace, her arms so softly around him, her long hair brushing against his cheek. Once, he'd thought he'd never want to leave the comfort of Sarah's arms. Now it only made him want to run.

"You look good, Nate," Sarah told him as she pulled away and sat back down. "It's so nice to see you back here. I can't believe you're home."

Nate nodded, thrust his hands into his back pockets. "It's—" he couldn't lie to her, not to Sarah "—different being back."

"I'm so sorry about your father." Sarah's eyes flooded with tears as she reached for him, her fingers curling around his forearm as she leaned forward again. "He was always so nice to me when I was here with you."

Nate smiled. He didn't even have to force it. "Yeah, he was pretty fond of you, too." Back in the days when he and Sarah were joined at the hip, his dad had loved him having Sarah over all the time. Everyone had, because there wasn't a person in Larkville who didn't like Sarah Anderson.

He looked up as she removed her hand from his arm and immediately wished he hadn't. Because he'd never forgotten the warm amber color of her eyes or the way she seemed to be able to look straight through him, to see what he was thinking, what he was feeling.

Only there was no way that even Sarah could know what was going on inside of him, not now.

Sarah sighed like she wasn't sure what to say, before turning a sunny smile his way. "Have you heard that I've been roped into organizing the Fall Festival?" Sarah shook her head. "I mean, I'm looking forward to the tribute for your dad, but trying to get everyone in this town into line is harder than it looks, I tell you!"

Nate couldn't help but smile back at her, and for once it was genuine, not him trying to act happy to get the people around him off his back. "I bet you're loving it."

Sarah glared at him, a playfulness there that had been missing in his life for so long he'd forgotten it had ever even existed. A spark of happiness that for a moment, the briefest of moments, made him feel like he'd never left the farm, never seen what he wished he could forget, never… Nate swallowed hard and tried to focus on Sarah's pretty face instead of the memories that haunted him.

"Are you home for good, Nate?"

Her question surprised him, made him crash back to reality. "Yeah." He grunted out the word, still unable to believe that after all these years his career in the army was over for good. That he was back home, and in such a short time he'd lost both his mom and his dad, too. Home sure wasn't what it used to be.

"You're certain?"

Nate braved making eye contact with the girl who had stolen his heart when he was a teenager.

"Yeah, I'm sure." He wished he hadn't snapped at her, but he couldn't help it. What did she want to hear? The truth of why he wasn't going back? Because not even Sarah could get details of *that* story out of him.

"I'm sorry, I know better than to pry." Sarah sighed again and looked away. "Moose!" she called.

Moose? Nate was about to ask her who the heck she was calling when… "What the hell?" Nate spun, ready to fight, body alert even though his leg was starting to throb.

"Moose!" Sarah called again, crouching toward the long grass where the noise was coming from.

A massive dog appeared, launching from his hiding place and landing in front of Sarah. Nate could have sworn his heart was about to beat straight from his chest and thump to his feet.

"Since when do you have a dog named Moose?" he asked.

The dog glared at him, sitting protectively beside Sarah.

"You know me, sucker for animals in need," she replied, stroking the dog's head lovingly. "Your brother found him one day and nicknamed him, because he looked like a gangly baby moose. No one knows how he ended up around here, but he's been with me ever since."

Nate eyed the German Shepherd, not liking the way he was being watched in response. The canine was acting like he was challenging his authority and Nate wasn't used to being the one on the back foot. "Is he as staunch with Todd as he's being with me right now?"

The smile fell from Sarah's face like water thrown over a flame at the mention of her husband.

"It was really nice seeing you, Nate, but we'd better be off."

He watched as she moved past him, her eyes damp again like she was about to cry. "Yeah, nice seeing you, too."

He should have asked her to stay. Should have patted the damn dog instead of acting like his territory was at stake. Because Nate was alone and seeing Sarah hadn't been half-bad. At least she hadn't quizzed him like his family had the moment he'd stepped foot on the family ranch again.

After so many years surrounded by other men, of living and working with other soldiers at his side, he was alone. His family were like strangers to him; he had no one to talk to, *no one he wanted to talk to,* and seeing Sarah had been the first time he'd cracked a smile in what seemed like forever.

But instead of calling her back, he watched her walk away. And it felt like they'd just gone back in time six years, when he'd told her that he was staying with the army instead of coming home. When he'd ended their relationship for good.

Sarah touched the top of her dog's head before sending him away in front of her. She tried to focus on him bounding ahead, tail wagging back and forth. But the only thing she could feel, the only thing she could think about, was the man standing behind her.

Nate Calhoun.

After all these years, seeing him for more than a fleeting moment was… Sarah dug her fingernails into her palm. Refused to turn around to see if he was still standing where she'd left him. Nate had been the love of her life, and no matter how hard she tried to pretend that there was nothing between them anymore, she was still drawn to him like a magnet to metal.

Why after so many years, after he'd left her, could she still not push the man from her mind? When he'd left her brokenhearted, discarded like their romance had been nothing more than a holiday fling.

"Sarah, what are you doing here so early?"

She looked up, forgetting how close she was to the homestead. The ranch house never failed to impress her, had always had a warmth and homeliness about it that she admired, even though it was easily one of the largest homes in Larkville.

"I came to check up on my new horse, but Moose ran after something and I ended up following him."

Kathryn Calhoun leaned against the doorframe, eyebrows drawn together. "What's wrong?"

Sarah sighed. It didn't matter how hard she tried to keep something to herself, she always seemed to wear her emotions all over her face. "I saw Nate."

Kathryn frowned. "Did you talk to him?"

"Yeah, but…" What did she say? That she still felt a flutter of something for him, even though she could see from the darkness in his gaze, from the drawn expression on his face, that the old Nate wasn't even in residence anymore? Twenty minutes ago she hadn't even known Nate was home and now…

"You don't have to tell me, I know," Kathryn told her.

Sarah's face flushed hot, but she bit her tongue,

waiting for Kathryn to continue. She liked Kathryn a lot, but it didn't mean she wanted to talk to her about her former flame, especially given she was married to Nate's brother, Holt.

"Sarah, he's changed. He's not the Nate his family knew, and he's not the happy-go-lucky town charmer that everyone seems to remember, either," Kathryn confessed.

Sarah was overcome with a burst of anger, wanting to defend him. "He's been through a lot, so don't we owe it to him to be patient? To give him some space to deal with being back here?"

Kathryn smiled at her, but there was a sadness there that Sarah couldn't miss. "I hope you're right, Sarah. I do. But Holt's not so sure that Nate's ever going to be the same again."

A wet nose thrust into Sarah's hand reminded her that she wasn't alone. "I think that's my cue to go," she told Kathryn. "I'm meeting Johnny to see how he's gotten on with my mare. He started her under saddle for me a few weeks ago."

Sarah waved to Kathryn as she turned, but the

smile fled her face as soon as she walked away. *Nate was hurting.* It might have been years since they'd been together, but she still remembered every expression his face had ever worn, how much pain he must be experiencing to hide away in the guesthouse, away from the family he was once so close to.

She threw a stick her dog had dropped at her feet and tried to focus on where she was walking, rather than the man she could see in her mind.

Nate had left her. Nate had walked away and decided not to come home. He wasn't her responsibility and he'd already made that perfectly clear.

So why was her heart racing like it was in a speedway competition, and her mouth so dry it felt like she hadn't consumed water in days?

Because it was Nate Calhoun, and for as long as she was alive she'd never, ever forget him.

CHAPTER TWO

NATE stretched his leg out and practiced some of the exercises he was supposed to be doing, in an attempt to relieve some of the pressure in his head. It didn't work. Instead, he ended up with a throbbing leg and his head pounded harder than before.

He needed to find something else to do, something to focus on, but right now it was too easy to sit under the tree in the shade and think. *And the fact he could see Sarah in the distance wasn't motivating him to move, either.*

He could see her talking to his sister Jess's husband. Johnny was clearly gifted with horses; he could tell that from watching him for only a few minutes. Sarah was leaning against the rail of the corral, one hand on the head of her dog, the other keeping her balanced. He was waiting to see her mount the young horse, to see if she was still as talented in the saddle as she'd been when they were younger. Back then, she'd been easily as good as any of the boys.

"Nate." A gruff voice commanded his attention.

He turned and looked up to see his brother standing behind him, fingers rammed through the loops of his jeans.

"Holt," he replied.

His brother stared off into the distance. It was obvious that he'd been caught out looking at Sarah.

"We see more of Sarah these days than we did for a long while," Holt told him.

Nate tried to act disinterested, but the reality was that he was anything *but* disinterested. Seeing Sarah again had made something within him, something he hadn't felt in a long time, stir to life again. No matter how hard he was trying to force it back down.

"She having her horse broken in here?" Nate asked. He knew from the letters Jess had sent him that her new husband was something of a horse whisperer, but he'd never had the chance to get to know him.

Holt dropped to his haunches, plucking at a blade of grass and avoiding eye contact. Suited Nate fine. The last thing he wanted was to be interrogated again.

"Johnny's giving her a hand. It's nice to see her smiling again."

Nate raised an eyebrow in question, met his brother's gaze when he looked up.

"You don't know about her and Todd, do you?" Holt asked.

Nate shook his head, slowly. "What do I need to know about her and Todd?" He hated the guy, even though he couldn't blame him. Sarah had married one of his best friends, and he'd never forgiven either of them.

"Look, Nate," Holt began, standing up again and fidgeting like the last thing he wanted was to have a conversation about Sarah and her husband. "Todd's out of the picture, that's all I'm saying. I thought you'd want to know, but if you want details, then I think you should ask Sarah. It's her story to tell."

Nate couldn't help the frown that took over his mouth. "So you're fine with telling me her marriage is over but you're not going to tell me what happened and why?"

Holt sighed. It wasn't something he remembered his brother doing often. "Nate, there's no reason to go jumping down my throat. I just don't think it's my place to tell you, okay?"

He swallowed what felt like a rock. Tried to channel his focus into the dull thud in his leg, anything other than ripping into his brother again.

"I'm sorry." Nate choked out the apology, knowing he'd been a jerk.

Holt held up his hands. "Yeah, I'm sorry, too. I just thought that if there was any unfinished business between you—"

"There's not," Nate interrupted, hearing the sharpness of his own tone.

He watched the expression change on his brother's face and hated that they were acting like strangers. Or maybe Holt wasn't doing anything out of the ordinary, but *he* sure was. They'd been as close as brothers could be once, had spent day after day together, been inseparable. Like his buddies in the army, Holt had always been there for him no matter what, and vice versa.

But now Nate had changed so much he didn't know if he'd ever be that brother to any of his siblings. Not ever again.

Holt walked backward, but he'd turned before Nate could apologize again, and he didn't even know where to begin, anyway.

So Sarah and Todd were over. He looked down and watched her, realizing it was she who was on the horse's back now. Elegant as ever, sitting straight and comfortable in the saddle, at ease with what she was doing.

He didn't need to know that Sarah wasn't spoken for any longer. He didn't need to watch her, or talk to her, or *anything* her now that he was back home. He had his family to deal with, twin siblings that he hadn't even met yet and a bunch of memories that kept him from slumber night after night after night.

Yet his legs were throbbing not from the pain right now, but from a desperate need to cross the field and seek out Sarah.

Just like he had as a lovesick teenager twelve years ago when he'd first seen her taking a riding lesson in the same corral she was in now.

Sarah nudged the young mare on. It was her first solo ride on Maddie, but she was responding beautifully, even leading the other horse beside them.

She gulped, trying not to think too hard about what she was doing. The last thing she needed was for Maddie to feel her nervousness and think it had something to do with their ride.

He was still there. The young man she'd known to never stand still for more than a moment, not able to stay in the same place because there was always something to do, was sitting where she'd left him, leaning against the tree like he had no purpose.

Sarah didn't bother calling out to him, because even though his head was down she knew he'd have heard her. Instead, she walked the horses straight over to him, never taking her eyes from his lone figure.

She'd been wallowing in her own self-pity, thinking she'd been hard done by. Seeing Nate and the change in him told her what she'd been through was nothing in comparison.

"Let's go, cowboy," Sarah ordered once she reached him, in a voice far more confident than she felt inside.

Nate's gaze made her smile wobble. It was as if a storm had brewed within him and was searching to exit through his eyes—eyes that had once been soft and loving now tumultuous and dangerous.

"You want me to ride?"

She held out the reins to the horse. It was one of Johnny's own, and he'd promised she'd be nice and quiet. Sarah had no idea how long it had been since Nate had ridden.

"It'll do us both good," she assured him.

Nate shook his head, before pulling his hat back over his short crop of hair, stretching and standing. "In case you haven't noticed," he said in a voice laced with ice, "I'm not exactly capable these days."

Sarah forced herself to look into his eyes, to not be scared off by his behavior. If he was trying to push her away, to make her scurry back to where she'd come from, then he was doing a darn good job. Except for the fact he was forgetting how determined she had to be with the kids in her classroom. Bullying and bad behavior didn't get her pupils anywhere, and just because he was a wounded soldier didn't mean he was going to get any special treatment.

"So you limp? I can see that for myself without you pointing it out, but I wouldn't have thought you'd let it stop you." Sarah's hands were shaking but she wasn't backing down. *This was Nate, for goodness' sake!*

"Sarah…"

"No, Nate, no," she insisted. "You can ride without stirrups, whatever, but I think it'll do you good."

He squinted up at her, his face showing the full force of his anger. "You been talking to my family?"

She thrust the reins down into his hands now he was closer. "Why, you been as rude to them as you're being to me right now?"

Nate's face crumpled, like a hard shell that had just been shattered, a snail dropped to the concrete from a bird's beak. "Damn it, Sarah, I'm sorry. I—"

She held up her hand to silence him. "There's

time for apologies later, Nate, from both of us, but right now I just want you to get back in the saddle."

Nate looked at her, stayed still for a heartbeat, before throwing the reins over the horse's neck and positioning himself on the left-hand side. She couldn't help thinking that he was lucky he'd injured his right leg, otherwise he'd have found it hard to mount, but she turned away before he caught her watching. Gave him a moment to right himself before she faced him again.

"No stirrups, you reckon?" he asked, a glimmer of the old Nate flickering in his voice.

Sarah shrugged. "Whatever's most comfortable. I thought we'd just go for a nice long walk, give this one a bit of mileage."

Nate's focus turned to the horse she was riding. "Young?"

"Yep, just started under saddle a few weeks ago, so she's doing pretty well," she told him. "I've had her since she was a baby, and now it's time to see if she's too much of a handful for me or not."

Nate pushed his foot into the stirrup on her side. She imagined he did the same on the other side or tried to from the grimace on his face, but he didn't say anything. Pushing his heel down would no doubt be painful, but until he was ready to talk, she wasn't going to ask. *Anything.* He'd tell her what had happened to his leg when he was good and ready.

"Tell me what you've been up to?" Nate was obviously trying to make an effort.

Sarah didn't want to talk about herself, had liked the neutral territory of horses. "Oh, you know, nothing out of the ordinary."

Nate looked sideways but his focus was clearly on the horse now.

"Have you ridden since you left?"

"Nope." Nate stroked one hand down the animal's neck. "I guess it's one of those things that you never forget how to do, though, right?"

"So I hear you're—"

"What do you—"

They both laughed. "Sorry," Sarah said with a laugh as they spoke at the same time. "You go first."

Nate looked like he was about to object, to tell her to go first, when his face visibly softened. Almost looked pained before he spoke.

"I hear you're no longer with Todd."

Sarah focused on the inhale and exhale of air as it whooshed through her lungs. She hadn't expected him to know. "You found that out between us talking earlier and now?" She had no idea who would have told him. "And here I was thinking you'd been sitting under that tree minding your own business all morning."

Nate's body visibly stiffened and he looked off into the distance. "It's none of my business, Sarah, you're right. I just wanted to tell you I was sorry."

Sorry that her marriage was over or sorry that he'd walked off and left her to marry Todd in the first place?

"It's fine," she lied, fixing a sunny smile on her face, not wanting to be drawn back into the past. "Todd and I weren't meant to be, that's all." She omitted the part about him running off with another woman who was already carrying his baby, about how he'd ripped her heart out with his lies and left her without a backward glance as if their marriage had meant nothing.

"So nothing else happening around here I should know about?" Nate asked her, clearly trying to change the subject.

"Other than the Fall Festival?" she mused. "Well, there's a few new people in town, but other than that, we're just the same as usual here in Larkville, I guess."

They rode side by side, far enough apart that there was no danger of them bumping knees, but close enough that it made talking easy. She noticed his foot was dangling from the stirrups now and she wondered if he'd done the same on the other side.

"Who knows about my twin siblings?"

Sarah bit down on the inside of her mouth, needing a moment to consider her reply. *Jess, Nate's sister, had told her about the secret Calhoun children and what had happened, but she hadn't expected Nate to bring it up out of the blue.*

"You haven't long found out, have you?" she asked him gently.

Nate glanced her way, made brief eye contact before fixing his stare forward again. "I wasn't contactable for a while, so I won't lie and say the news didn't come as a shock when they finally tracked me down and told me."

Sarah swallowed, uncomfortable. "Not everyone knows, but I've seen a lot of your family lately, and Ellie and I have become great friends. She's wonderful, Nate. I think if you gave her a chance you'd really enjoy her company. Maybe not as your sister straightaway, but as a nice friend at least."

He laughed. A cruel laugh that she didn't recognize. "Right now I can't even spend time with the siblings I grew up with, so what makes you think I'd do any better with a stranger?"

"Don't talk like that, Nate. Just don't." Tears flooded Sarah's eyes but she refused to let them spill over. She'd promised herself years ago that she'd never shed a tear over Nate Calhoun ever again, and just because the circumstances were different didn't change anything.

"I think we should head back," he announced, turning his horse in the direction they'd come in.

Sarah halted her horse and paused a moment before following him, whistled to her dog to call him over. This wasn't the Nate she'd known, and it sure as hell wasn't a Nate she could ever have imagined returning home. Sarah tried to quell the anger rising within her, anger toward Nate that she'd long held in check.

If she wasn't on a newly broken horse she would have cantered off with her head held high and left him, but with the way her mount was starting to dance on the spot beneath her, she wasn't going to push her luck. Not on her first ride.

Sarah trotted after Nate's retreating figure and contemplated pushing him clean out of the saddle. A smile played across her lips. *Returned wounded soldier or not, a slap across the cheek and a shove off his horse was probably exactly what Nate needed. Not that she'd ever be that game.*

"Nate, wait up!" she called.

He didn't stop, but she could see the slight turn of his head telling her he'd heard her.

"This is stupid," she told him.

"What is?" he asked, a scowl crossing his face. A face that even with a more weathered appearance, with soft crinkles alongside his eyes and faint dark marks beneath his bottom lashes, was still ridiculously handsome.

"You behaving like this, us acting like nothing has happened one minute, then you clamming up the next."

She could see the tautness in his jaw, that he

was probably grinding down on his teeth, a hollowness in his eyes that she wished wasn't there. "I'm not the man I used to be, Sarah. That's the truth of it, and there's nothing I can do to change that."

Sarah shook her head, sadness flooding her again. "I don't believe you, Nate," she told him. "I know you've seen awful things, that you're struggling with something right now and that you've been injured, but I believe the old Nate is still in there. Somewhere." She sighed, forcing herself to continue. "I don't know what happened to you over there, Nate, but don't give up on yourself yet. Okay?"

Nate didn't respond and she was too choked up to say anything else. So they rode in silence. Him on his borrowed mount, her trying to keep up, and her dog running along beside them without a care in the world.

Nate knew he'd been rude to Sarah, and she didn't deserve it. But he was all out of apologies, of trying to figure out the right thing to say. When all he wanted was to be left the hell alone.

He cleared his throat, knowing he needed to say *something* before he lost his chance and she walked from the barn and out of his life again for good. He'd already pushed her away once, and he didn't need another black mark on his conscience.

"Sarah," he started, running a hand through his longer than usual hair.

She stopped and turned to him, her face tilted up to look him in the eye. Next to him she seemed tiny, fragile. In reality she was tall and willowy, but in flat boots she seemed much shorter than he remembered.

"I, well, I'm not myself right now, Sarah. I didn't mean to snap at you before, but I can't deal with any of this. Okay?" Nate knew it was a terrible apology, but it was the best he could come up with right now.

"I know you're hurting, Nate," she responded,

closing the distance between them to touch his arm, to tighten her fingers against his skin.

He looked into her eyes, into deep amber eyes that had haunted him for years…in his sleep, while he was awake, when he had nothing else to do but think about what he'd left behind in his determination to fight for a greater cause, to serve his country in the absolute best way he could.

If only it was someone as sweet as Sarah who haunted his nights now. No longer dreams, but nightmares that relentlessly kept him awake night after long night.

"Nate?" Sarah was still touching him, her grip heating his skin.

He untangled himself. He had no other choice. Sarah touching him was too real; he didn't want to feel human again, preferred the dull deadness he'd become used to. He didn't want to acknowledge how kind she was being to him when he knew how badly he must have hurt her.

"I'm here for you, Nate. If you want to talk, if you need anything, don't be a stranger."

Sarah's eyes were kind, the smile kicking up her lips so pure that he wished he had the guts to grab hold of her and not let her go. To fold her slender body against his and cradle her, to remember what they used to have, the man he used to be. To make him feel less like damaged goods and more like a human being again.

"Thanks," he managed, his voice a husky octave lower than usual.

Sarah's fingers skipped across his upper arm and she left, walked from the barn leading her young mare, ready to turn her out in the field again.

Nate stared after her until she disappeared, eyes caught by the softness of her silhouette. Slim-fitting T-shirt, worn jeans that she obviously found comfortable to ride in and that darn dog sticking close to her like he viewed Nate as an imminent danger.

Would she still use her maiden name? Nate

forced the question from his mind, trying to re-focus on the horse he was supposed to be brushing down.

So she was single again? What difference did it make to him? Nate had made a choice six years ago, and as far as he could tell, there was no going back from that.

Not now and not ever.

Sarah pulled out a chair from the table and dragged it across the room. She stood on it, rummaged around in the high cupboard and yanked out what she'd known to be hidden there.

She shouldn't be looking at it, not after all these years, but seeing Nate had brought back a flood of memories that she couldn't help but want to revisit. When she was married to Todd, she'd done her best to put the past behind her, but now...

Sarah smiled as she flicked to the first page. Hearts doodled in pink pen, Nate's name written in curly letters that she'd thought were fancy at the time. There were pictures of them on the ranch and hanging out with friends, notes he'd written her back when they'd been in class. *She'd kept them all,* even after she'd married Todd and they'd moved in together, when she'd known they should have been forgotten about.

She turned to the last page, needing to wipe the smile off her face by reminding herself why they'd broken up.

Nate had looked so handsome that day, dressed in his uniform, cheeky smile on his face as he'd turned toward the camera.

They'd made promises the day he'd left to each other, promised that they'd find a way to stay together no matter what. She'd never wanted to hold him back, *but then he'd always promised he'd come home.* That they'd do whatever it took. Instead, he'd broken her heart, and made her realize that waiting for him had been a big mistake.

Sarah flipped the tattered book shut and left it on the table. Maybe she'd show it to Nate, maybe she wouldn't, but now he was back there was no use trying to run from the past. She'd loved Nate with all her heart, and maybe, just maybe, she'd never stopped.

Sarah walked into the kitchen and made straight for the cake she'd made earlier. She had planned on giving it to Johnny for helping her out with her horse, but she needed a sugar fix and fast.

And not for the first time, she wished she wasn't such good friends with the Calhoun family. It wasn't like she could talk to them about Nate, not when it sounded like he wasn't even on speaking terms with them himself.

CHAPTER THREE

NATE took a deep breath. He wasn't used to being nervous, had spent years being the brave one no matter what the situation, but right now he was knee-shakingly worried.

He raised one hand and knocked lightly on the door, not wanting to alarm his sister or her new husband.

The door opened, only halfway, and Nate looked down to see a little boy with messy blond hair. *His nephew.* For some reason he hadn't expected the boy to answer.

"Hey, Brady." Nate could almost feel his blood pressure dropping from being confronted by a child instead of his little sister. She might be younger than him, but she could be darn bossy, and he was still wondering if he'd done the right thing in turning up. But he couldn't hide away forever, and he was lonely. After so many years in the army, he was equal parts miserable about being alone and relieved not to have to pretend like he was okay to his buddies.

"Tell Holt that he can't keep sneaking in the front door and stealing my chutney!" Jess called out.

Nate smiled. So Holt was still taking Jess's things without asking. Some things never changed. Maybe he *had* missed them.

"Mom, it's not Uncle Holt," Brady called back, grinning as he grabbed Nate's hand and tugged him into the kitchen. "It's—"

The kid didn't have a moment to get the word out.

"Nate!" Jess dropped what she was doing and rushed around the counter to him. "Johnny, turn the television off."

Nate shook his head. "No, don't make a fuss. I just thought I'd take you up on that offer of dinner. If you have enough to spare, that is?"

"Enough to spare?" Jess gave him a hug, her slender arms wrapping right around him, before she pulled back and kissed his cheek. "We always have more than enough to share, especially for my favorite brother."

Nate gulped, pushing away the feeling that he should have stayed home alone. But he couldn't stay there forever, and if he was going to try to make amends, then Jess was the person he wanted to start with. She was his youngest sister, and even though she liked trying to fix other people's problems, for some reason he'd come to her instead of going up to the main house.

"So I'm your favorite brother now?" he joked.

Jess responded with a slap to his arm, followed by a tight, impromptu hug.

One step at a time, or at least that's what he was trying to keep telling himself.

"Nate."

He clasped hands with his brother-in-law, forcing a smile. Nate had nothing against the man, was pleased his sister had found happiness, and he seemed like a good guy; it was just that he wasn't ready for small talk again yet. Especially not with someone he didn't know.

"I hope you don't mind me dropping in like this?" Nate asked Johnny, releasing his palm and stepping back, shoving his hands into his pockets.

"I know all about wanting to be alone, so you can come here whenever you want," Johnny told him, slinging an arm around Jess's shoulders. "This one here might try to talk your ear off, but—"

There was a soft tap at the door followed by the creak of it opening. Before Nate could raise an eyebrow at his sister, ask who they were expecting, or even turn, he caught sight of the grimace on Jess's face.

"Are you…?" Nate didn't even get to finish his sentence.

"Sarah," Jess said with a smile, nudging him on the way past. "I was just about to tell Nate that we were expecting company for dinner, and here you are."

Nate looked at Sarah, at the frozen expression on her face, and then surveyed the room. He should have realized when he'd arrived that something was up. The table was set with pretty napkins that he was certain wouldn't be used on a nightly basis, and even Brady was dressed nice, not in clothes dirty from an afternoon playing outside.

"Nice to see you again, Nate."

Sarah's soft voice pulled him from his thoughts. He had no place being rude to her, giving her the silent treatment, so this was going to have to be his chance to redeem himself.

"You've already seen Sarah since you've been back?" Jess asked.

"I found Sarah under my tree this morning," he told his sister, still not taking his eyes from the woman standing in the entrance to the room, cake held out awkwardly in one hand, bottle of wine clutched in the other.

"Nate, please don't tell me you've forgotten your manners."

Nate laughed. Jess sounded just like their mom. Bossy but saying her words with a smile so it sounded less like an order than it was. He crossed the room and took the plate from Sarah, giving her what he hoped was a warm smile. "Sorry," he muttered.

Sarah looked up, her amber eyes lighter than he'd remembered, her cheeks pink like she was as embarrassed as he was. Nate turned before he stared at her any longer, trying to ignore the way her dark auburn curls brushed her shoulders, or the low scoop-cut of her T-shirt.

"The cake looks, ah, great."

Sarah laughed. "It should do! It's the second one I've made today."

Nate looked over his shoulder to see his sister take the bottle of wine and follow him into the kitchen. Brady was talking flat-stick to Sarah, already dragging her by the hand to the sofa.

Jess prodded him in the back.

"Ow!"

He got a soft kick to the calf in response. Clearly his sister didn't care about him being injured. "It seems a little convenient that you've only just come home and yet you managed to find Sarah sitting under your tree already. Is that why you showed up here tonight?"

Nate crossed his arms over his chest as Jess moved around to stand in front of him. "Give me a break, Jess. Maybe I should have just stayed home." He was tempted to wave them all good-night right now and leave them to their dinner, and that was before his sister had started to interrogate him.

"All I'm saying is that Sarah's been hurt enough this past year without you coming here and doing the same. Again."

Nate closed his eyes and took a deep breath. He wasn't ready for dealing with this kind of thing, not yet. He didn't have the thoughts inside his head in order, hadn't dealt with what was troubling him, so he couldn't take on anyone else's troubles.

Besides, it was she who'd been sitting under his damn tree!

"I would never hurt Sarah, you know that. And I'm not interested in her that way, not anymore."

Jess shook her head. "You've hurt her before, Nate, and anyone can see the way you two still look at each other."

She was wrong. Jess was way off the mark with that comment. "Do you want me to go?" he asked.

Jess set down the bottle of wine she was still carrying and marched him into the living room. "You're not going anywhere, Nate. It's about time you came back to your family."

Nate groaned. Maybe he should have gone up to the main house, after all. If he was going to make an effort, Holt might have been easier to spend an evening with, and his new wife would surely have been easier on him than Jess was.

* * *

Sarah was struggling to engage in conversation. Heck, she was struggling to breathe, so it was no wonder she couldn't speak! Nate was sitting quietly on the other side of the table, his eyes still stormy but without the anger she'd seen flashing there earlier.

"Sarah, would you like some more?"

She locked eyes with Jess, who was staring at her with a smile on her face. Sarah tried hard not to blush, but she'd been caught out watching Nate and now everyone was looking at her. Even little Brady had stopped his chatter.

"Maybe just a little," she murmured, focusing on spooning more of the chicken and rice dish onto her plate. "It really is great, Jess. I'll have to get the recipe from you one day."

Nate chuckled. "I think you'll find that there's not a recipe as such."

Sarah relaxed as the burning heat receded and left her cheeks at a more comfortable temperature. "Sounds like there's a story behind this dish, then?"

Nate straightened and leaned forward slightly, the first time he'd actively engaged without his sister prompting him. Everyone else was silent.

"Mom made this for us when we were young, even though she always moaned about how many chickens she needed to fill us all."

His smile made Sarah grin straight back at him. It was so nice to see that flicker of...*Nate.* Him being like this reminded her of how he'd been years ago. Before everything had changed.

"We used to beg her for this every birthday, special occasion, you name it, even when we were growing up," Jess continued, rising and dropping a kiss to her brother's head as she passed him. "She never did have a recipe for it, because she'd tasted something similar in a Chinese restaurant and this was her trying to replicate it."

Sarah looked at Nate again. There was a frown starting to drag the corners of his mouth down, but she could see he was trying hard not to pull away from them.

"When Mom died, when I could have thought of so many things, I thought about this," Nate told them, shaking his head as he pushed his fork around his plate. "One of the first things I thought was that I'd never eat her chicken and rice again. Stupid, I know, but I was so damn hungry at the time, sick of eating crap food where I was posted, that I could almost smell the chickens roasting in her oven. Could see myself sitting in her kitchen as she cooked up a storm around me."

Sarah couldn't help it, she reached across the table for Nate's hand. He didn't resist, and she needed to touch him. Needed to comfort him when he was so clearly lost. She should have been angry with him, but right now all she could feel was his pain.

"When she confessed to not having an actual recipe, I started to watch her every time she made it," Jess said, taking over the storytelling.

"I used to cook it for Dad sometimes, to remind him of her, and now I can cook it for all of you when we need a little pick-me-up."

Sarah had no idea how she'd ended up sharing a meal with Nate after all these years, being part of his family again. She moved her hand away from his, but not before squeezing gently.

The look he gave her, the powerful way he seemed to stare straight through her, sent a soft tickle down her back, and she didn't look away.

Right now, it was like a glimpse of what could have been. *If Nate had come home, if he'd never left, they could have been sitting around this table every week. But the one thing that wouldn't change was that there'd be no little Nates sitting with them....*

Sarah glanced at the food on her plate, the extra spoonful she'd only just added, and knew she couldn't eat it. She stood to help Jess clear the table instead, needing a moment away from Nate. Away from the happy family scene that she'd been enjoying so much until her silly fantasy had taken over her thoughts.

It didn't matter that Nate was home, and there was no point even thinking about what could have been. Because the truth was he'd made the decision that he didn't want to be with her when he chose not to come home. And the perfect little family they'd often talked about when they were together? It wasn't even possible.

No matter how badly she wanted children of her own, that wasn't in her future any longer. There was nothing she could do to change that, and she sure didn't want Nate to know about it, either.

"Do you want to cut the cake or shall I?" Jess called out.

Sarah hurried into the kitchen and took a deep breath, relieved to be away from the table even for a moment, before taking the knife and starting to slice into it. "I'm fine doing this, you go and sit down," she told her friend.

She'd already eaten enough cake to make her

stomach ache earlier in the day, yet her brain was trying to tell her she was ready for more comfort food already.

Sarah spun around with a plate in each hand before dropping one with a smash to the floor.

"Nate!" She'd run smack-bang into him, the plates bumping straight into his chest.

He bent to scoop up the fallen slice of cake with one hand, the other collecting what was left of the broken plate.

"I'm sorry, I…" Sarah didn't know what to say, so she put the other plate on the counter and bent down, too, picking up the smaller fragments.

Nate's hand hovered close to hers, so close she wished he'd touch her, to feel his fingers against her skin. Like a drug she'd long given up but was so overwhelmingly tempted to consume again.

"Everything okay in there?"

"Fine," Nate called back to his sister.

Only Sarah wasn't so sure things were fine. Her heart was beating hard and fast, and her stomach was flipping at a rapid rate. She held the broken pieces of plate in her hands before braving a glance at Nate, and finding him looking straight back at her. His blue eyes icy as he stared.

"Sarah." He stated her name, like he wanted to say something else but couldn't figure out what or how to go about it.

"Do you want to go for a walk?" Sarah's question came out as a whisper.

"Now?"

She nodded. Nate plopped the cake on the remainder of the plate he held and offered her his arm, careful to keep his sticky cake fingers away from her. Sarah accepted his help but didn't look him in the eye again. Didn't connect with him or touch him in any other way, because she was starting to feel so out of her depths, so weak, that she was terrified.

They both rinsed and dried their hands in silence.

"Jess, we're going for a walk," Nate told his sister, calling out but not moving. "Be back soon."

Sarah followed his lead, heading out the back door. And when his fingers brushed hers, the most gentle of touches as they walked together, hands hanging at their sides, she didn't pull away. They curled against her own, fingers so close to interlinking they were halfway to holding hands, before the moment was over and she was left with a shiver crossing her shoulders as the wind touched her bare skin instead.

CHAPTER FOUR

NATE buried his hands deep in his pockets to avoid doing anything with them he'd regret. What was he thinking, reaching out to Sarah like that? He hadn't just come home to his sweetheart and he needed to remember it. But the pull toward the woman beside him was almost impossible to ignore.

"I'm sorry if I ruined your night."

Sarah's softly spoken words made Nate stop walking. "What's that supposed to mean?"

She wrapped her arms around herself, like she was trying to shield her body from danger. "When I arrived and saw you there, I don't know…it just felt like I was intruding. And I know you haven't seen much of your family since you've been home."

Nate started to walk again. He didn't want to do this. Didn't want to talk about his feelings, or why he was so distant with his family, or how conflicted he felt being here with her right now. *Or why it somehow felt right, either.*

Because the truth was he was still angry with Sarah. Even though he knew he'd played his part in what had happened, that he'd been the one to end things, she'd taken a piece of him when she'd married Todd.

Just like Jimmy's death had taken a piece of him, and his parents' dying had smashed away another chunk that would never grow back.

He was a broken man and he knew it.

"No one seems to realize what I've been through, Sarah, and that makes it kind of hard to relax around here." Nate looked away, wondering if he shouldn't have been quite so honest. "I don't feel like I fit in anymore, that I'm part of anything that's happening here now."

Sarah didn't give him time to think about it. She was at his side, hand clasped around his wrist, tugging him around. Not letting him continue.

"How can they know anything about what you've been through if you don't explain that to them?" she asked, her voice low.

He wished he wasn't staring into her eyes, wished he could ignore what she was saying and walk away, but he couldn't.

"Sarah, I can't go there," he told her, his voice rough with the honesty of his words.

She didn't break eye contact with him. "Can't or won't, Nate?"

Nate faltered, a lump of emotion forming in his throat and threatening to choke him. "What happened over there, what I've…" He stopped talking as abruptly as he'd started. "I'm sorry."

Nate walked away, because he didn't need anyone seeing him like this, seeing the way he couldn't deal with what was going on in his own head. Didn't need to relive what had happened, not again. *He already did that every time he shut his eyes.*

"Nate." Sarah was in front of him again, blocking his path, the gentle way she said his name making him turn.

Then she did something he really hadn't seen coming. She thrust her arms around his neck, pulling him in tight for an embrace he was powerless to evade. Held him like he hadn't been held since the last time he'd seen his mom, the kind of hug that forced his body to relax and be comforted. The kind of hug that would once have made him feel loved.

"You're home, Nate," she whispered in his ear. "You're home and you need to remember that. Home is where the heart is, and that's right here on this ranch with your family."

He didn't know if it was the smell or feel of Sarah in his arms, the safeness of being cocooned by her, or just being held by another human being, but Nate was fighting a losing battle.

When she tipped back, looked up at him for the briefest of moments before pulling away, he did something he'd thought about for longer than he could remember. Something that he'd never forgotten, a memory he'd never let go.

Nate reached out to stop her, his palm tucked to the back of her head, holding her in place. *And then he kissed her.* Brought his mouth toward hers before she had a second to see it coming, to resist him, and touched his lips to hers.

Sarah sighed into his mouth, slipped her hands around his waist, pillowy lips brushing like the softest of feathers against his. Mouths grazing together in the most gentle, intimate of dances. Until she pulled back like she'd only just realized what had happened.

"This doesn't mean I forgive you," Sarah said in a low voice, slowly removing her hands from his waist and crossing her arms across her chest instead.

Nate swallowed hard and looked down at Sarah. She looked tiny yet brave at the same time, stronger than he'd probably ever given her credit for. He wished he could snatch her hands back and plant them on his hips again, but he fisted his own hands at his sides instead.

"For the record, I don't forgive you, either." And he didn't, it was true. Forgiving her or not had nothing to do with kissing her. That was something he'd *needed* to do, and it had sure taken his mind off everything else that had been troubling him.

"I think we should head back," Sarah told him, angling with her head over at Jess's house. They had walked a short distance away, but even in the pitch-black the house was clearly visible. Lights illuminating every window, glowing as if inviting them to enter.

It was the sort of homely scene that should have tugged him back into the life he'd once yearned for. The life that he'd imagined going back to once he'd served his country, before everything had changed forever.

Nate tried not to let his pain show as he walked beside Sarah. Sometimes it was the pain within him, the pressure in his head, the stabbing betrayal and loneliness that constantly hurt him, far worse than the physical pain in his leg.

"So are you here riding again tomorrow?" Nate asked Sarah, needing to break the silence more to get away from his own thoughts than to fill the air around them with words.

Sarah smiled, shyly, and he knew she'd be blushing if only he could see her cheeks. It was dark now, but still light enough that he could make out her features.

"It's summer vacation for me, so I'll be riding as much as I can over the next month."

Nate nodded. "You love being a teacher as much as you always thought you would?" He'd always remember how much Sarah loved children, how she'd always wanted to be a teacher in their small town, taking all the younger ones under her wing. Children had always flocked to her like a honeybee to pollen.

"It can be hard work, probably harder than I ever thought it would be, but there's nothing more rewarding that I could imagine doing," she told him, walking faster than before.

Nate laughed, finally starting to relax in her company. "All you're missing are the four kids of your own, right?"

The smile fell from his face as Sarah's arms wrapped around herself again. She didn't make eye contact, acted like she hadn't even heard what he'd said, or like he'd said something he should have kept to himself.

"I'm sorry," he said, running a hand back and forth through his hair. What the hell had he been thinking, saying something like that? "Just because Todd wasn't the one doesn't mean you won't have everything you dreamed of one day, Sarah."

She faced him, stopping just ahead of him, a tight smile greeting him as he watched her face. "Not everything turns out the way we want, Nate. We both know that."

Nate tried not to grind his teeth, tried to ignore the discomfort of what they were suddenly talking about even as it drilled through his body. *Once, there were so many things he'd have said to Sarah. So many things he would have apologized for, promises he could have made. But not now. Once, he'd have known why his words had stung her like they so obviously had, too.*

"You're right," he said, instead of any of the other thoughts going through his mind. "It was nice seeing you again, Sarah. If you wouldn't mind telling Jess for me that I've called it a night, I'd really appreciate it."

He continued to stare at her face, seeing the hurt that he was powerless to do anything about.

"Goodbye, Nate." Sarah shook her head, just the barest of motions, but she didn't turn away.

But he did. Before she told him something he didn't want to hear, or he said something he'd only regret later. Nate walked away, knowing that he needed to get back to the guesthouse, to be alone to deal with what he needed to think through.

Alone.

He repeated the word in his mind until he heard Sarah walk away, too.

Sarah fiddled with her keys. She'd been jangling them in her palm since she'd left the house, and now she was standing beside her car trying to make a decision she shouldn't even be considering.

What was it about Nate Calhoun that still made her twist up in knots like this?

Sarah sighed and decided to drive as close as she could to his place and walk the rest of the way. She had a piece of cake wrapped up that she wanted to give him, since he'd missed dessert, and for some reason she wasn't sure that he was in the right frame of mind to be left alone.

He wasn't her problem anymore, but she still wanted to help. Because she knew what it was like to be left, to deal with secrets and feel like there was no one in the world who would understand. She needed to keep swallowing her anger, wait until the right time to confront him with her pain, with her questions. *And that time wasn't now.*

Sarah parked her car less than a minute's drive away from Jess's place, and walked quickly toward the small house Nate was staying in. There was only one room illuminated in the dark, the window coverings pulled to mute the light, but still enough for her to see the way.

What would he be doing? Watching television, reading a book, staring into space?

Sarah summoned all the courage she could muster and raised her hand to knock on the door. There was no answer. She tapped again, harder this time, wishing the door wasn't made of solid timber so she could look in and see if he was there. Peer in and make sure she'd made the right decision in coming here instead of driving to the safety of home. As far away from Nate as possible.

She went to knock again before the door was flung back, nearly sending her spiraling forward into the house.

"What do you…?" Nate's angry question trailed off when he saw her.

Sarah stared at him, unsure what to say. He'd been crying. *Nate had been crying.* The same Nate who she'd never seen cry in all the years she'd known him. His eyes were bloodshot as he swiped his face with the back of his hand, trying to remove any evidence of the tears she'd seen sticking to his skin.

"Nate, if this is a bad time…" she managed.

His dark laugh sent shivers across her skin. "It's always a bad time for me lately."

She wondered who he'd thought it was when he'd opened the door as angry as a disturbed, hibernating bear. But she knew that if he truly wanted to be left alone, if he enjoyed being locked away from the world as much as he was pretending to, then he never would have answered the door.

Sarah held out the piece of cake. "I just came past to give you this on my way home."

Nate took the dessert, raised his eyes and

stood back from the door. "Good night, Sarah. Thanks."

She walked backward and jumped slightly as the door shut. *What the hell was she doing? Nate was crying and she hadn't even tried to comfort him.*

Sarah marched back up to the house with a determination she'd thought had long departed. She went to knock, changed her mind and swung the door open instead.

It was warm inside, that was the first thing she noticed when she stepped in, until…*oh, my.*

Nate's head was in his hands, his shoulders hunched, body crumpled like it was broken. Sarah took a deep breath and crossed the room, falling gently into the sofa beside him. She tucked one arm around his shoulders, hugging him tight.

"Go away, Sarah." His voice was muffled, strained, as he tried to push her away.

"I'm not leaving you, Nate," she told him, pulling him tighter.

He shook his head, face still hidden by his hands. "I don't want you to see me like this. I don't want anyone to see me like this," he mumbled.

Sarah resisted the urge to touch his hair, to run her fingers through it or trace the edge of his face and pull his hands away. Instead, she stayed still and took a deep breath.

"Nate, you can't keep doing this alone."

"After what I did to you, why do you even care?" He raised his face, straightened his shoulders and looked at her. He'd cried so much that she could see a damp line across the top of his T-shirt, his eyes still full of tears she'd interrupted, waiting to fall but instead left in residence against his dark lashes.

"Just because I care doesn't mean I have any interest in you romantically," Sarah told him, trying her hardest to keep her voice even. Technically, her response to their kiss earlier would prove her a liar, but she wasn't ever going to admit how good it had been to get up close and personal to her former flame again. "Yeah, I'm still angry with you, Nate, but right now that's not what's important."

Nate stared at her, like he was questioning her without saying anything.

"I need you to leave."

"No," she replied defiantly.

He fell back into the sofa. "Why? Why won't you just leave me the hell alone?"

Sarah bent forward and wrapped her arms around the man she'd once thought she'd marry. "Because you're stubborn and you need a hug and someone to talk to."

Nate laughed. Despite the terror and heartache she'd seen in his eyes when she'd first walked in, and the pain she could see within him still, he laughed at her.

"Can we skip the talking and just drink coffee instead?"

Sarah let go of him and edged her bottom backward, her fingers curling against the edge of the fabric beneath her. "How about I get that coffee brewing?" she suggested.

Nate looked as unsure as she felt, although she doubted his insides were flipping as fast as hers were. Like her stomach was a pancake being turned constantly in a frying pan.

She had no idea why she was here, why she was torturing herself with Nate's company. Because they were never going to have a second chance, and she was never going to have the future she'd dreamed of, with or without him.

"Nate?" Sarah asked as she rose.

"Yeah?"

"You can still tell me to leave if you don't want me here." Sarah kept her eyes down, not looking up until his fingers hooked under her chin, forcing her to look at him. At the man she'd thought only moments earlier was broken but who now looked like life was slowly seeping back into him, his gaze brooding and fierce.

"Maybe I was wrong. Maybe you're exactly what I need right now."

Sarah jumped up, broke the contact before she had the chance to relax into his hold.

"Good, then I'll get that coffee we talked about."

Nate watched as Sarah crossed the small living area and stepped into his kitchen. *She still took his breath away.* Even a war-hardened cynic like him couldn't deny how beautiful she was. *But he needed to block out any thoughts of why he found Sarah so attractive, because that kind of thinking was going to get him nowhere fast.*

"Where's your dog tonight?" Nate had no idea why he was thinking about her animal, but he didn't want her neglecting her dog for his sake.

"In the car," she called back.

He watched her move the coffee cups closer to the fridge, before reaching in and pouring milk into each one.

"I guess you better go get him, then."

Sarah laughed at him, her entire face changing as she clearly tried to stop herself from making fun of him. "Are you sure about that? I'm not convinced you two got off to the best start this morning."

Nate glared at her, but the plain simple truth was that her being here was already helping. Had somehow pulled him clear of the darkness he'd been falling headfirst into when she'd opened his door.

"How about you go get him, then? Have some bonding time together, work out your issues," she suggested, still grinning.

Nate headed for the door, wishing he could think of something to say back, a joke even, but struggling. He felt better, but still not himself, if he even knew who *he* was anymore. Sarah had just seen him at rock bottom, *or maybe not true rock bottom when he considered where he'd been these past few months, but bad enough for him to feel embarrassed about what she'd witnessed before.*

He'd never let anyone see him cry before, not

like that. *Not ever.* But maybe the only way he was going to get better *was* to let someone in.

Nate kept walking, spotted her car as his eyes adjusted to the dark. But with his head full of thoughts about the woman in his house, about what he could talk to her about and what he couldn't, he didn't hear the person creeping up on him until it was too late.

The crunch of a footfall, too close for him to avoid, made his body tense. His muscles screamed, senses heightened as he switched from hunted to predator.

Nate spun in a deadly turn and grabbed his attacker, all in one swift motion. He was blinded by desperation, not prepared for the neck he clasped in one hand to feel so smooth, for the body to be so light as he swung it to the ground and landed astride his attacker.

Damn!

"Sarah, I'm sorry. Oh, my God, oh, no, Sarah…" Nate removed his hand from her neck like a snake had bitten him. *What the hell had he done?* Tear-filled eyes looked up at him, the terror on her face so obvious Nate could hardly breathe. "Sarah, Sarah…" he choked out her name.

"Nate," she whispered. "I'm sorry." It didn't sound like her voice, was so meek he wouldn't have recognized it if he hadn't been staring straight into her eyes.

"*You're* sorry?" he whispered back, forcing his legs from either side of her, before crouching and collecting her to him like she was the most precious of dolls. "I could have killed you, Sarah. I'm…" He kept all the expletives locked in his mouth.

"It's okay, Nate. I shouldn't have snuck up on you like that."

He could feel her body shaking, like a leaf trembling in the worst of a winter's storm. "Please don't tell me what I did to you just now is anything close to *okay.*" He took a deep breath, forcing himself to keep his feet planted in the soil beneath him. Nate gently, *so gently,* touched her throat with his thumb, stroking it. "How bad does it hurt?"

She wrapped her palm around the delicate skin at her neck, forcing his hand to drop away. "It'll be fine. Honestly, Nate, I'll be fine. You let go pretty quickly."

Nate was listening but he wasn't. There was no way any part of this was fine, or that she wouldn't be traumatized by what he could have, what he *had,* done to her just now. She was brave, he'd give her that, but she was also stupid not to be angry with him.

Nate turned away and took another deep breath, trying to deal with the situation as a soldier, not as a messed-up guy who'd just flattened an innocent woman. *A woman he'd once loved.* He wanted to tell her that he needed a moment, that he needed to be left alone to think, but what he needed to do was pick up the pieces of what he'd done, to make sure Sarah was as okay as she was claiming to be. *Even if all he wanted was to run.*

"Let's get your dog and then take you back inside," he suggested, trying hard to keep his voice even, to not let any of the anger surging through his body infiltrate his tone.

Sarah nodded, but she didn't move closer to him until he put his arm around her, forced himself to touch her even though he was terrified of holding her close. "I would never hurt you, Sarah. I am so, so sorry." Nate blew out a big breath.

She relaxed and let her head rest against him, like she was trying to prove that she wasn't frightened. "I only wanted to give you my keys," she said, producing them from her pocket. "I locked Moose in."

Nate took the keys from her and steered her toward the car, sucking back a breath and forcing himself to say something to ease the tension he'd caused. "I hope that dog didn't see what happened back there, otherwise he might eat me alive."

Sarah laughed, but from the nervous trill of

noise she made, Nate knew she was feeling as on edge as he was. He could have seriously hurt her back then, and then what would he have done?

Because dealing with what had happened this year was enough pain and guilt to last him a lifetime.

CHAPTER FIVE

NATE was surprised that the dog had relaxed in his house, but he had no intention of letting his guard down, or making another mistake when it came to Sarah. The way he'd behaved earlier… He involuntarily shuddered. It made him sick that he was even capable of doing that.

"I think we need to move on to something stronger," he told her, holding up a bottle of whiskey he'd found in the pantry.

Sarah's eyebrows met as she gave him an uncertain look. "You want to drink?"

"The way I'm feeling right now isn't exactly lending itself to cups of tea or coffee." Nate had never been a drinker, but after everything that had happened it was exactly what he needed tonight. But the way Sarah was looking at him, like he was some sort of a wild man, was making him think he should skip the JD and just pour himself the cola.

"Just one," she said, still not looking convinced. "I have to drive so don't go making it too strong."

"On the rocks?"

She rolled her eyes and he added cola to the second glass, before putting a handful of ice in both. Clearly she wasn't any more used to drinking than she had been as a teenager.

"Nate, you're not, um, well…" Sarah took the glass he offered her and shuffled back into the sofa. It was the only place to sit aside from the small table in the corner, so he sat at the other end.

"What?" he asked.

"You're not drinking regularly, are you?" Her words came out in a jumble and her cheeks flushed red.

"I have plenty of problems right now, Sarah, but hand on my heart I've only had the odd glass of wine with dinner since I…" Now it was him faltering, his sentence trailing off instead of hers. "This is just soda." He held up his glass.

"Since when, Nate?" she asked. "You were about to say something."

He watched her hand as it cupped the glass tight, kept his gaze trained on her delicate fingers. "Since I left the recuperation facility."

If she was shocked she didn't show it. "So you weren't serving up until you arrived home."

Nate revisited his choice of drink, poured just a small nip of whiskey over some ice and slowly swallowed, grimacing as it burned a slow, steady trail down his throat. "If I tell you this, you need to promise to keep it to yourself." He wasn't even sure he wanted to tell Sarah, but it was killing him not having anyone to talk to, not being honest with anyone around him. "I haven't told my family any of this." Not that he had any intention of telling her *everything*, but even getting just part of his story off his chest would be a relief. "Except for my shrink, but given what happened earlier I think I need some more regular sessions."

Sarah's eyes were wide but he knew he could still trust her. "We spent years confiding in each other, Nate. I didn't share anything you told me then, and I have no intention of doing it now."

He refused to think about the past he'd had with Sarah. Because right now he needed a friend, and if he thought about the way things had ended, what had happened... He forcibly pushed it from his mind.

Nate crossed the room again to collect the bottle of liquor. He tipped a little more into her glass, deciding not to top up his own. But he couldn't sit down, not now, not with what he was about to tell her. Instead, he paced slowly back and forth.

"When I found out about Dad passing away I was still serving, but when the news came to me about the twin siblings we'd never known existed? I was already back in the U.S." Nate took another sip of his drink, trying to ignore the shake in his hand. He thrust the other in his pocket in case Sarah noticed it. "I'd asked my superior not to alert anyone to the fact I was back on home soil."

"Why did you want to keep that a secret? Your family would have loved having you home earlier than expected."

Nate laughed, but he could hear the cruel edge to it, was powerless to react in any other way. "Because I wasn't capable of dealing with anything then. What I've been through, Sarah…" He raked a hand through his hair, tugging at it in his frustration. "I needed time out and I didn't want anyone else to know that I was struggling or what I was struggling with. You've got to understand that I went from loving what I did to resenting it, and now I'm stuck somewhere in between."

They sat in silence, but he could tell that Sarah was thinking. She reached down to stroke her dog's head, like she was biding her time.

Nate went back to sipping his soda for something to do.

"When you injured your leg, did something else happen?"

Nate tried not to react, to keep his face expressionless. *He wasn't going to tell her the truth about his injury, about what had happened that day, because talking about it would only mean reliving the experience all over again.*

"The past couple of years I've been part of Black Ops," he admitted. "I was recruited as a part of an elite squad and we had an operation go bad. After my injury, I spent a few months in a recuperation facility without my family being alerted, because I was considered *at risk.*"

He knew that Sarah would be desperate to know more, to understand more of what had happened and what he'd been through, but she nursed her drink without asking him another question.

"When you're ready to talk about it, Nate, you only have to say the word and I'll be here."

He nodded. "I appreciate that." Not that he had any desire to open up about anything else.

"So how about we make a toast to your dad?" she suggested.

"Good idea." Nate leaned forward and poured a small portion of whiskey into his glass. "To Clay Calhoun."

"To Clay," she agreed. "But, Nate?"

He raised an eyebrow in question.

"If we're going to keep drinking I might need some more cola. It's getting a little strong."

Sarah was in over her head. Way out of her depths. But she didn't know what to do.

Nate was in need of a friendly ear, some company while he was down, so she could hardly leave him. But a few more sips of alcohol and she wouldn't be able to drive home.

"What happened between us, Sarah?"

His words sounded blurry. She took another sip of her potent drink.

Did they have to be having this conversation now?

"Nate, I think we just need to let the past stay in the past. What happened to us…" She had no idea what to say to him. "It just happened, okay?" Stay down, she ordered in her mind. Now was not the time to get angry with him.

His face lost all expression as he sunk back farther into the sofa. "It didn't just happen, Sarah. I made a bad decision. *Bad decision after bad decision.*"

Sarah's pulse started to race, her heart beating faster than she was comfortable with. Since when did Nate admit to being wrong about something? But going back in time wasn't something she was convinced they needed to do, not with alcohol to fuel the situation.

"You left me when I thought we had something special, something worth fighting for," she told him, knowing she had to at least be honest.

"And you ran straight into the arms of Todd when we'd barely been broken up for a day," he fired back, anger screaming from his rigid body. A vein had risen on his forehead, one fist was clenched, and the other hand looked in danger of crushing the glass he held.

"You know what? I'm sorry, Nate. I'm sorry for marrying your best friend and I'm sorry for whatever the hell happened to you these past few years." Sarah reached for the bottle and poured herself another nip of whiskey. "But don't forget that *you*—" she pointed at him "—were the one who ended it. I was waiting here and you told me it was over."

He sighed and reached forward, skimming her cheek with his fingers before taking the bottle from her. "He wasn't my best friend, Sarah."

She stared at him. "But—"

"You were," he interrupted. "Todd was a good friend but you were my best friend. There was never any doubt in my mind about that."

Tears stung Sarah's eyes; her throat was so tight she found it hard to breathe.

"It's not your fault, Sarah, you're right. If anything, when I left Black Ops it made me realize I'd prioritized all the wrong things in my life. It's been one major screw-up after another."

Sarah turned her head slightly so Nate couldn't see her face, and brushed away the tears hugging her lashes. "You're a highly decorated soldier, and you've just told me you were in a special forces team. You've hardly been a screw-up, Nate."

He shook his head. "On paper, I've had it all. In reality?" He looked down into his glass. "I lost you, I lost my best friend from the army and now I've lost both my parents. Nothing has turned out like it should have."

"You lost a friend?" She'd known something had happened to him, that there was more than just an injury playing on his mind, something that ran deeper that he'd been unable to open up about before. She put down her drink, wishing she hadn't kept sipping away when it wasn't something she was used to doing.

"Yeah," he grunted. "We met the first year I

served and we were recruited into Black Ops together. And now he's gone, too."

Sarah opened her mouth to ask more, but Nate's tearful shake of his head stopped her from pushing further.

"To your friend," she said, raising her glass instead.

"To fallen comrades," he agreed, holding up the bottle and taking a long sip.

Sarah did the same and then laid her head back on the sofa. The last time she'd drunk like this she'd probably been with Nate. And back then it had probably been Nate who'd convinced her it was a good idea. Just like now.

Nate opened his eyes slowly, one at a time. It seemed to help the thumping in his head.

What the hell had...oh.

There was a reason he'd woken up so comfortable, before the sunlight had hit his vision and forced him to shut his eyes again.

Sarah lay half-curled up over him, her hair

splayed out over his lower chest and part of his stomach, one arm slung across him. He tried not to smile at her faint snore.

Snore or not, though, Sarah was beautiful.

In the years he'd been away, even when he'd hated her so much for marrying Todd, when he'd known he'd never be able to forgive her, he'd always remembered her like this. And she'd hardly changed a bit in all these years. Not to look at and not to be around.

Her hair wasn't quite as long as it had been when she'd left for university, but it still had a slight curl and fell below her shoulders. Nate tried to resist touching it but he couldn't. He ran his fingers through the silky strand touching his chest, stopping himself from stroking her face. *She wasn't his anymore, and she never would be.*

Nate removed his hand and shut his eyes again, not wanting to ruin the moment but needing to keep at least an emotional distance from the woman still asleep on him.

And then he realized.

Last night had been the first night since Jimmy's death that he'd slept without waking. Without writhing, covered in sweat, reliving every moment of what had happened to him. Of what had happened to his friend, of firing over and over at the machine gun nests that had come so close to ending his life.

Jimmy looked at him. Made contact with his eyes—eyes that were so filled with pain Nate had found it hard to return the stare—before holding his gun up and starting to fire.

The silence that had engulfed them all, that had kept their presence hidden from the enemy, turned into a constant ricochet of gunfire. A noise that had filled Nate's head and made it hard for him to focus.

Until he'd realized that it was Jimmy. That it wasn't the enemy but his best friend firing like a crazy man, before turning the gun on himself.

Nate had run, had moved faster than he'd ever known he was capable of, but it was too late.

Jimmy gave him one last look, before Nate could push the gun away, before he'd squeezed the trigger and taken his own life.

Nate had been hit, the bullet slamming into his leg like a blasting ball of fire, but he'd dragged his friend away. Managed to get him back to safety and fire at the enemy simultaneously, doing his best to ignore the spasms of pain.

Only it had been too late.

Was it Sarah or the booze that had given him a night's peace? Because it was always the same every time he shut his eyes, and he'd never imagined it would ever stop. Not that he'd even drunk much, except for a few good swigs from the bottle when Sarah had started to fall asleep on him.

"Nate?"

Sarah's sleepy voice pulled him from his thoughts and forced him to open his eyes again.

"Morning," he replied, watching as she fought to extract herself from him before one hand shot to her head.

"What did you do to me?" she moaned. "How did I end up…?" Sarah opened her eyes again, looking horrified. He watched as she glanced down, then at him. "Did we drink all of that?"

Nate followed her gaze. An empty bottle lay on the floor close to where her dog was still stationed. Asleep.

"I think it would be fair to say that you consumed more than me," he told her.

"This is all your fault." Sarah stretched, then slowly moved off him. "And my head is pounding."

"Ditto."

Nate laughed, then stopped himself. He'd gone one night without waking up in a sweat and now it was suddenly okay to joke around? *Not a chance.*

"Todd's coming back into town today," Sarah told him as she straightened her top and pushed at the creases in her jeans like she was nervous and didn't know what else to do, or maybe she was making sure she hadn't removed any of her clothing. "He wants to discuss some things and get me to sign the divorce papers. So he can marry his fiancée."

Nate swallowed an imaginary lump. What? "Did you just say fiancée?"

Sarah gave him a tight grin. "Yup, he's moved on pretty fast. I just wish I could shock the pants off him and make him realize that him leaving did me a favor."

His hands fisted at his sides, anger rising fast within him. "Tell him you're marrying me, then," Nate said, wishing Todd was in front of him right now so he could show him just how pissed off he was with the way he'd treated Sarah.

Sarah let out a big hiccuping laugh. "I thought I was hungover, but I must still be drunk." She stared at him. "Oh, my God, you're serious, aren't you?"

Nate knew it was stupid, but right now in the mood he was in he'd do anything to protect Sarah. "You want to show Todd you're doing fine without him, and I want to get my family off my back. It's a win-win situation for both of us. We could just pretend for a while, watch out for each other."

Sarah had gone from confused to angry. Fast. "No, it's a stupid idea, Nate. I've already had one failed marriage, and I don't want to lie to anyone."

"Okay, stupid idea," he agreed. *What the hell had he been thinking, anyway?* The last thing he needed was to complicate things. "I'm not thinking straight, but what I do know is that I need a break from my family and I want to help you."

"Why?" Sarah asked, standing beside her dog now, even though her head must have been throbbing as hard as his was.

"Because I owe you one, Sarah. I owe you a favor for the way I hurt you, and because I need your help."

"Why can't you just be honest with your family? At least tell them what you told me?" she asked.

Nate folded his arms across his chest, as if he

could squeeze the pain away by just hugging himself. "Because there's a whole lot more to my story than I'll ever be able to share with anyone, and I need some time on my own. Away from questions and too many people thinking they can save me."

"You're wrong about one thing, Nate." Sarah's voice was low.

He waited for her to tell him what she was talking about.

"You *can* be saved, and if I'm going to help you out with your family? Then I'll be making sure that *saving* you is my number one priority."

Sarah wished she knew the truth about Nate. About what had really happened that had messed him up so bad. She glanced back up at the main house again, her cheeks burning at the thought that someone might see her sneaking away from Nate's place.

"Mornin'."

Sarah squeezed her eyes shut and took a moment. Just a nanosecond to gather her thoughts. How had Johnny snuck up on her like that? And on a horse? She must have been way too deep in thought for her own good.

"It's not what it looks like," she blurted, wishing she didn't sound and feel so guilty.

"None of my business." Johnny tipped his hat, a big grin on his face. "I just thought I'd check in and see if we're still riding later?"

If it was possible to die of embarrassment, Sarah would have dropped on the spot. "Yep, sure. I'll see you later on," she mumbled, scurrying to her car.

She'd thought the whole town knowing about Todd leaving her for another woman was embarrassing, but being spotted leaving Nate's place this early in the morning, in the same clothes she'd been wearing the night before? Hands-down worse than anything about her marriage breaking down.

Sarah opened the back door of her car, realizing how Johnny had known she was here. "Come on, Moose, up you get, bud."

The dog leaped in and she flopped down behind the steering wheel. Her head was still pounding, and her mind was a scrambled mess. On the one hand, it was nice not thinking about Todd anymore, but having her mind stuck like a broken record on Nate Calhoun wasn't exactly doing her any good, either.

CHAPTER SIX

NATE chugged back another glass of water in an attempt to leech any remaining alcohol out of his system. He wasn't convinced it was working, but he hoped a walk around the ranch would do him some good. Take his mind off the pounding ache of his mind working overtime, and give him some time to think about how the hell he'd gone from miserable and unable to talk to anyone around him, to opening up to Sarah and ending up asleep with her on his sofa.

He was still miserable. How could he not be? If it wasn't his leg giving him grief it was the memory of what he'd seen, the reality of the life he'd lived up until now.

His nostrils felt like they were burning, and his eyeballs, too. So much smoke, so many rounds fired...it was like dreaming of hell and not being able to wake. But he knew it was reality, because the screaming of his muscles from carrying the heavy frame of his friend was too real to be a nightmare.

Nate wished he could run, to see if he could somehow escape his mind when it raced off like that back into the past, but all he could do was limp. And wish to hell he'd have done something to save his friend's life before letting things go so far.

He glared down at his leg like it was to blame for what had happened. It was a constant daily reminder of what had happened, the bullet fragments that couldn't be removed stuck there forever.

What he needed was a horse to ride, and he knew exactly who to ask for one. If Johnny would lend him a mount for a couple of hours, maybe he'd stop feeling so helpless and sorry for himself. At least he could still ride—he'd figured that out when Sarah had insisted he haul himself up in the saddle the day before.

Nate walked as straight as he could down to the home field where he knew he'd find the man he was looking for, but no matter how hard he tried, he couldn't stop his fingers from finding a now-crumpled piece of paper buried deep in his pocket. A letter he'd been sent when he'd first arrived back in the States, passed to him by his superior and with him ever since.

Lucy. His friend's wife, and the woman he'd been meaning to contact ever since the full military funeral he'd attended in his best friend's honor. Then, he'd been on crutches and a complete mess, barely able to say a word let alone recount what had happened to the grieving widow. But now he knew he owed her at least a phone call, to answer her questions and tell her how sorry he was. To do his best to tell her how much she had meant to the man he'd trusted with his life on so many occasions over the past four years. How much Jimmy had meant to him, too.

Only picking up the phone wasn't going to be easy. Because Nate knew that if he'd intervened, if he'd done what his gut had told him was right, then Jim might still be alive today. He might not be remembered as a hero, he might have serious issues to deal with and be pretty messed up, but he might be alive if Nate had spoken up and done something.

Instead, he'd lied for the man who'd been his best friend. And that lie had cost him his life.

Sarah had never been so pleased she'd worn makeup into town. She always made an effort to look nice, but today she'd worn a pink polo shirt that she'd never even taken the tags off before. Usually her riding attire consisted of a favorite T-shirt and worn jeans, but knowing there was a possibility of seeing Nate when she returned to the Calhoun ranch had made her spend longer getting ready than usual.

She stayed sitting in her car as she watched a familiar figure walk out of Nan's Bunk'n'Grill.

The woman beside him wasn't so familiar, probably because she'd been shuddering with rage the one time she'd seen them together, but her husband sure was. *Soon to be ex-husband,* she corrected.

What was Todd doing back here with her? He was only supposed to be coming back to gather the remainder of his things and have a discussion with her over their settlement and divorce. There'd never been any mention of him bringing his fiancée, and he'd told her he wouldn't be arriving until late in the day and driving back the same night.

So long as he was still okay with her keeping the house and him taking everything else, though, she wasn't going to be complaining. But both of them here? Her head was still killing her and her stomach was worse than delicate. She didn't need to be dealing with any of this right now, not when she was trying so hard to make a fresh start.

Seeing them together was only going to add

to her nausea. And it wasn't because she still loved him, or that she was bitter about being lied to, because truth be told she'd known for a long time that her marriage wasn't working—that Todd wasn't right for her—but she'd been too darn loyal to make the decision to leave him when she'd thought he loved her.

She was upset because of the damn baby bump his new girlfriend was sporting. When all she'd ever wanted was a family, when she'd tried with Todd ever since their wedding night to conceive.

And now he was about to become a dad and she was never going to become a mom. Not with him, not with anyone else. Not ever.

A tap on her window sent her sky-high, fingers clasping the steering wheel as if it was going to save her from an intruder.

Sarah looked sideways and saw it was only Mrs. Sanders. An older woman she'd known since childhood, bending down and looking in at her like whatever she wanted to talk about couldn't wait a moment.

She plucked her bag from the seat, glanced at Todd walking down the road away from her and opened her door.

"Hi, Mrs. Sanders. How are you?" Sarah did her best to sound bright and cheery. Knowing that Todd was back in town wasn't exactly helping her self-confidence—she hated the thought that people she'd known all her life could be talking about her marriage, or lack of. Or worse, pitying her.

"Well, dear, I wanted to ask you about the Fall Festival."

Sarah stifled a groan. She didn't mind a task to keep her busy, but right now she didn't want to be making small talk over the festival that she was *trying* to take a couple of days away from planning.

"I think there are a few things that didn't go as planned at the last festival, so I have a few suggestions to discuss with you," Mrs. Sanders told her, leaning in close like she was divulging a grand secret. "I'm sure you want it to be perfect, too, don't you, dear?"

Sarah did sigh this time. She couldn't help it. She definitely didn't need to be told what to do today, and she certainly didn't want to spend all morning discussing the festival or anything else for that matter. Today she just needed some time to gather her thoughts.

"Mrs. Sanders, I'm in a bit of a hurry this morning, but I'd love to hear your thoughts," Sarah answered politely. "There's a meeting at Gracie May's for everyone involved on Sunday night, so if you'd like to come along then, we can all listen to your suggestions. We're going to have supper while we run through everything."

She watched as the other woman struggled not to continue, clearly bursting at the seams to vent her thoughts. "Well, if you don't have a moment right now…"

Sarah raised her hand in a little wave. "I'll look forward to seeing you on Sunday," she said firmly as she walked away. She fought pangs of guilt gnawing in her gut. Usually she'd have stopped and given anyone her time freely, but she was starting to feel like too many people were taking her willingness to help time and again for granted.

Sarah fought not to let her shoulders slump as she searched the street with her eyes. She'd lost track of where Todd had disappeared to and she didn't want to bump into him. Not now when she wasn't prepared.

She might feel prettier than usual, but seeing Todd wasn't on her agenda.

Nate's words echoed through her mind as she walked into the store. *You can help me with my family and I can help you with Todd.*

She wasn't usually one for playing games or keeping secrets, but after seeing Todd before, it was starting to sound like an appealing option. Not Nate's ridiculous idea to say they were getting married when she wasn't even divorced yet, but maybe to something…

But could she cope with seeing more of Nate?

She knew in her heart that she hadn't ever forgiven him, and maybe she never would, but with everything that was going on with her right now? Helping Nate transition back into civilian life would give her something meaningful to focus on over the summer break, and she wanted to help him so bad it was like a constant bruise to her heart. Anger aside, they'd once meant a lot to each other.

"Sarah?"

She looked up and realized she'd been in such a daydream she'd almost walked straight past her own mother.

"Mom! Just the person I need to talk to."

Her mom cringed and laughed at the friend she was talking to. "Oh, dear, that's my day gone."

Sarah took her mom's arm and propelled her to the checkout. She needed someone to talk to, and fast, and the last place she wanted to do it was standing in line at the grocery store.

"Who or what's got your knickers in a twist?"

Sarah grinned. She wondered if her mom

would have used that phrase if she'd known what she was about to tell her after all she'd seen her go through in the past with the man in question.

"Nate's back in town," Sarah told her mom later over the table at dinner.

"Nate Calhoun?"

Sarah felt like a teenager talking about her first date. "No, another Nate."

Her mom raised an eyebrow at her like she didn't appreciate being made fun of. "It's nice he's back again. Is he just here for the festival? To do something for the commemoration on his father?"

She took a sip of her coffee. "It sounds like he's back for good." The thought struck terror through her body—just saying it aloud made it real. It was such a small town, and if Nate was back here to live, then she'd be seeing a lot of him, whether she wanted to or not.

"You're not thinking of—"

"No!" Her mom didn't need to finish her sentence for Sarah to know what she was about to say. She wasn't thinking about Nate like that; she would never think about rekindling what they had had...*or would she? That kiss...* She shut her mind off.

"Just remember that I was there when he left, when he promised that he was coming back for you and when he didn't. When he—"

"Forget I said anything," Sarah interrupted. "It's just that I saw him yesterday and with everything that's going on and what he's been through, it left me a little confused."

Her mom looked at her long and hard before clasping her hand and pressing a kiss to it. "You and Nate were wonderful together, sweetheart, and you know how much I loved him, but don't forget how hard you fell back then. You know I adored him, too, but you both went in such different directions and I don't want to see you hurt like that again, especially after everything you've been through lately."

Sarah moved around to the other side of the

table to sit beside her mom and give her an impromptu hug. "Ah, who could forget my impending divorce." She made a face. "Maybe I should just forget men for good."

"Now Todd, he's a different story. At least Nate didn't *mean* to hurt you," her mom pointed out. "Whatever happened between you two, there was never any doubt in my mind that Nate loved you, and I know that calling things off must have hurt him more than he probably realized."

Sarah held up her hand and shook her head. "Let's not even get started about the fact that they both left me or I might start to get a complex. And as for Nate hurting me back then? It was his decision and I still haven't forgiven him."

She hadn't missed the fact that she'd faced a whole lot of heartache in the relationship department in the past few years. So maybe even seeing Nate again as friends was taking things too far.

And that kiss... Argh. It kept popping back into

her mind at the worst of times, her lips tingling as if it had just happened only a moment earlier. *Anger.* What had happened to her anger?

"Thanks for the pep talk, Mom, but I'd better go. Did I tell you that I rode Maddie for the first time yesterday?" Sarah took her chance to change the subject.

Her mom smiled. "That's exactly what you need. Out on horseback, just enjoying yourself."

Maybe she wouldn't tell her mom exactly where she'd been riding or with whom....

Nate grimaced as he swung his leg over the saddle. He was starting to get used to the ongoing pain, but sometimes when it twinged like that it still managed to take him by surprise.

"You all right?" Johnny called out.

Nate tipped his hat and nudged the horse forward with his inside leg. "Yep, thanks for the loan." He liked that his brother-in-law had left him to his own devices. Nate made a mental note to tell his sister how much he approved of her new husband.

He tried to force his heels down in the stirrups but it hurt too bad, so he took both feet out instead and tried to relax. He was back on the land and he should, here of all places, feel at peace with his surroundings.

Nate needed to clear his head and work out what the hell he was going to do. How he was going to readjust again. Because while the rest of his family were busy thinking about the upcoming festival and moving on with the realization that they had siblings they'd grown up without knowing, that their dad had had a whole other life before he'd married their mom, Nate wasn't.

Because *his* mind was full of disturbing memories, his nostrils still filled with the acrid smell of too many guns firing at close range when he least expected it, and his leg ached every time he thought about his friend. Like it was somehow linked to his memory and what he'd lost.

Nate crossed his stirrups over the horse's

wither so they wouldn't hit him in the ankles and nudged the horse into a trot and then a canter straightaway. He didn't fancy bouncing around at the trot, but he'd be darned if he couldn't still canter without stirrups and keep his balance.

He'd grown up riding horses as soon as he could walk and followed his dad around the ranch on horseback whenever he could as an older boy. So right now, the place for him to be was in the saddle. He needed to reconnect with the part of his past that didn't haunt him, remember how he used to feel at home, surrounded by his family.

Sarah had been right. Maybe not about him needing to talk, but about him riding and being out on the land again. Because he wasn't one of those guys who'd joined the army to be part of something. He'd loved it for that reason, but he'd grown up with a great family of his own, and he'd left here to make a difference, not to run away.

Sarah. Last night she'd momentarily reignited

something within him that had been dead for months, but he couldn't act on it. She'd married his buddy and now she was most likely heartbroken and looking for a rebound kind of relationship.

And he wasn't about to be that guy. Because he'd loved Sarah with all his heart once before, and he had no intention of going there again. No matter how much he was craving her after kissing the hell out of those plump lips of hers the night before.

Sarah felt like her head was about to explode. Not from suffering the effects of too much wine anymore, but for how long it had taken her to get back in her car and to the Calhoun ranch. Organizing the festival was starting to become more work than she'd bargained for. Putting everything together wasn't the hard job, but dealing with so many old-timers with set views on what should and shouldn't happen was starting to wear her down. Especially when they seemed to seek her out wherever she went—another had accosted her on her way back to her car!

But now she was here she was starting to unwind again.

Every time she was in the saddle, it was as if the stress was sucked away and her mind was clear. Having her young horse started during her divorce was possibly the best thing she could have done.

Sarah gathered up her reins. "You ready to let off some steam, Maddie?" Sarah whistled out to her dog and urged her young mare forward. "Canter on!" she commanded.

She fought the urge to shut her eyes as the wind whipped at her vision. *And it wasn't just the wind.*

Seeing Todd before had brought everything back to her, made her wish so hard that it was she who was pregnant. It wasn't Todd she was grieving; it was the knowledge that she'd never be able to carry her own child, never be able to be the mom she'd dreamed of being all her life.

Her horse shied out beneath her and Sarah did her best to stay seated.

She swallowed a curse. *That was precisely why she needed to concentrate on riding and stop thinking about her problems.*

"Whoa, girl." She reached a hand down to rub Maddie's neck, letting the reins run through her fingers a little on one side. "You're okay," Sarah soothed. She coaxed Maddie on, only trotting now but trying to prove to her that there were no hidden bogey monsters in the trees they were approaching.

Only, her horse had been right. There was someone there.

Sarah sat back deeper in the saddle and pulled slightly on the reins to slow her mount to a walk. There was a horse tethered nearby, which must have been what had originally spooked Maddie, and a man asleep in the canopy of shade cast by a large tree. And from the length of the jeans-clad legs, and shape of the body attached to them, it was…damn it. It was Nate.

She could have kept riding and pretended like she'd never seen him, but she wanted to stop. They'd spent the evening before in each other's company, and she had no reason not to stop.

Other than the fact that she was hurting and had been on the brink of tears less than a minute ago, and seeing Nate again had brought back a whole heap of feelings that she wasn't keen on reexploring. Just when she thought she'd come to terms with her infertility, seeing Todd and then being around Nate had stirred it all to life again.

Sarah halted her horse and tethered her near to the other one. She seemed calm enough, no longer jumpy, so she left her and walked closer to Nate.

No matter how much she'd tried to hate Nate for leaving, for ending all the plans they'd made and dreams they'd once shared, she'd never been able to. She'd cried over him, cursed him and hated what he'd done and what had happened between them, but she'd never been able to *hate* him. Never been able to rip up the photos of them as a couple, either, or forget about what being with him had felt like. Angry, sure. But hate? *Never.*

Now he was back, nothing seemed to make sense. If Nate had never left they still wouldn't have been able to fulfill their dreams, because everything they'd planned to do one day involved a family. *Something that wasn't possible for her, no matter who she was married to.* Her doctor had made that blatantly clear.

And seeing Nate now… His legs were crossed at the ankles, sturdy boots protruding from his faded denim jeans. Nate had his cowboy hat over his face to block the sun, and her fingers itched to pull it away. So she could stare her fill, look at his full lips and strong cheekbones, drink in that chiseled jaw covered in what she imagined would be a sprinkling of stubble.

Sarah started when Nate moaned—made a series of noises that sounded more animal than human. His body started to shake, then he started to murmur, words coming from his mouth that sounded like apologies, like he was asking someone to stop, then whispering *no* over and over.

She couldn't just stand over him and watch him suffer, but she had to be careful. After his reaction yesterday when she'd walked up behind him in the dark… The memory of his hands around her throat and his heavy body pinning her to the ground made her shudder. He could have hurt her bad, but she still knew she had to do something.

Sarah slowly dropped to her knees and touched a hand to Nate's chest, over his heart. Bent to whisper to him, to coax him awake so he'd know she was there and she wouldn't give him a fright.

"No!" His scream echoed out at the same time as he sprang into action, grabbing her arms and flipping her onto her back before she had a chance to avoid him. Nate's eyes were wild, his grip tight. *Too tight.* Like he had no idea what was going on or who he was.

"Nate!" she begged. "Nate, it's me." Her voice

came out as a terrified whisper, her wrists burning as he held her down. *Please, not again.*

"Sarah?" The life came back into his eyes as he focused, his eyebrows creasing in the center, forming an arrow. "Sarah?" he asked again, like he knew who she was but couldn't figure out how they'd ended up like this or what he was doing to her, why he was holding her down.

"Nate, please," she begged, trying hard not to cry. "Let me go."

It took a moment, a slow moment as he seemed to realize what he was doing and what he had to do. When he did, his hands moved with lightning speed and he scrambled back, on his haunches, a few feet from her. The look on his face was pure terror—horrified of what he'd just done to her.

Sarah sat up, wincing as she rubbed gingerly at her wrists. Nate had hurt her this time more than she wanted to acknowledge, and from the disgusted look on his face, the last thing she needed to do was make him feel any worse than he already was. Not again. *He couldn't help what he'd done, but he'd sure scared the hell out of her.* What he needed was professional help, not her losing it over his actions.

"I'm sorry." His voice was low, almost pleading.

Sarah threw him what she hoped was a convincing smile, trying not to let him see how much it had affected her. "I shouldn't have snuck up on you like that. It was just that…"

"I was dreaming," he finished for her, looking up, his eyes more haunted than she could ever have imagined them looking.

"Exactly," she confirmed. "So what happened just before wasn't your fault."

"It doesn't make me any less ashamed," he snapped, standing and staring off into the distance. "I could have hurt you, Sarah. Really hurt you this time." Nate shook his head. "For the second time in two days, I could have done something else I'd regret forever," he mumbled.

She shrugged even though she knew he wasn't looking. Did he mean something else when he said *forever?* "I don't believe that." Even with her wrists aching and her heart still racing, she hadn't truly feared him before. Not to the point where she didn't want to be near him because she knew he'd realize what was happening before it was too late. "You scared me, Nate, but you stopped yourself." She moved closer and reached out to touch his arm, gently trying to coax him into turning around. "That's all that matters."

"Don't try to downplay this, Sarah. I woke up and I thought you were part of my dream. I could have…" He turned back to her, shoulders slumping as anger crept back into his tone. "Damn it, Sarah, I could have snapped."

"But you didn't," she said straight back, not wanting to think what exactly he meant by *snapped*. "You didn't and I'm fine." She was the one being stubborn now.

He glared, eyes flashing. "Sarah, I don't know what you want me to tell you, or what the hell you think you're doing here, but I'm not the guy you used to know. I'm *nothing* like him any-more, so I think you'd better go."

His anger, the hatred in his voice, made her recoil like she'd been slapped. Where had that come from? What was making him so angry, *at her?* She was the one who had a right to be angry with him, for *everything,* not the other way around.

"Nate, don't talk like that," she said, wishing she could do *something.* Anything to shoulder some of the pain he was suffering, to try to help him when he needed it most.

"You can't fix me, if that's what you think, Sarah. I'm not one of your school pupils having a bad day. A cup of hot chocolate and a cuddle isn't going to make me feel better, *so just go.*" His voice was low, rumbling with enough anger to startle her.

"No," she fired back, losing the fear that had temporarily taken over and fighting back in-stead. "You don't get to talk to me like that, and you don't get to act like you're a lost cause, either. You hear me, Nate? You don't have any right to be angry with *me*."

He laughed. He actually had the nerve to laugh at her! A cruel, painful growl of a laugh as he stared her down.

Nate turned away, then whirled back around, closing the distance between them, his huge body blocking her path, looking down at her like he was about to explode. "I have nightmares every single night, Sarah. Every time I shut my eyes, I relive the horrors of what I've been through, and I thought for once that sleeping in the daytime, out in the open, I might actually be able to avoid waking up and thinking I was back in the depths of hell," he told her. "So when I tell you to leave me the hell alone, I mean it. Because no one can help me, not you and not anyone else around here. *Are we clear?*"

Sarah pressed her fingernails deep into her skin as she crossed her arms, refusing to blubber even if he did have her shaking in her boots. Literally. She'd never in her entire lifetime been spoken to like that—it was far more terrifying than what he'd done to her before. *This wasn't a man she knew, and she was starting to doubt it was a man she wanted to know, either.* Regardless of the past they'd once shared.

"The only thing we're clear on, Nate, is that you're nothing like the man I used to know." Sarah refused to break their stare, not willing to back down no matter how much she wanted to collapse into a trembling mess. "Because the Nate I knew would *never* have spoken to a woman like that, and he sure as heck wouldn't have spoken to *me* like that."

"Well, the Sarah I thought I knew would have waited more than a night after we broke up before jumping straight into bed with one of my best friends," he snarled. "So maybe we don't know each other as well as we thought."

Sarah burned with fury, her entire body alight with more emotion than she'd ever felt before. Her hand rose before she could stop it, slapping Nate with a flat palm across his cheek.

She snatched it back in a motion as fast as the act itself, horrified by what she'd done.

Nate just stared down at her, as motionless as a statue. His expression never changed, and he never said a word.

"Let's not forget that you ended our relationship, Nate. You told me it was over and I dealt with that the best I could. So don't you *ever* act like I was the one in the wrong."

Sarah turned and walked away from him. There were words she could have said, but she didn't. Because Nate wanted to be left alone, and the way she felt right now meant he'd sure made his point clear.

Tears pooled in her eyes, the second bout of tears she'd had to blink away within an hour, but Sarah never looked back. She reached her horse, mounted and rode away.

He could have called out to her, or come after her, but if he did she never heard him.

Sarah's palm still stung where she'd hit him, but she knew she deserved the pain. She hated violence, in any shape or form, and she couldn't believe she'd slapped Nate like that. Even if deep within her, she knew that he damn well deserved it.

Nate touched his cheek. He didn't care that it was on fire still from where Sarah had slugged him with her open palm, but he did care why she'd done it.

He'd behaved like a jerk. Said things that he never should have brought up, looked at her in a way that wasn't fair. Putting all his fear and anger into words that Sarah shouldn't have ever heard…but maybe she was right. The Nate Calhoun of old was gone, and right now he didn't even believe in himself enough to think that one day he might return.

Once, Sarah had been the most important person in his life. The person he'd imagined growing old with. Back then he would never have imagined speaking to any woman like that, let alone someone he cared about.

Nate roared. He roared like a wild bear with a thorn imbedded in his paw, before slamming his fist into the massive tree behind him. His hand exploded into a thick burst of pain, so intense that it sent him reeling. He collapsed onto the ground and cradled his hand, lying back with his eyes shut.

He didn't even know who he was anymore. Because the man he'd thought he was? It was as if he was gone and had lost all connection to the life he'd once led.

Nate cringed as he tried to move his fingers, forcing them to open and close.

Maybe it would be best for everyone if he just up and left. Because being back home was starting to hurt worse than being away had.

CHAPTER SEVEN

NATE glared at the computer screen but it didn't do him any good. The army physio wasn't going to go easy on him, which meant his only option to get rid of him was to shut the screen on his laptop. Given the circumstances, he doubted that would be the best option, and besides, there were other things he needed to discuss with him.

"Two more sets and we'll call it a day," the doctor told him.

Like he'd read his mind.

Nate grunted as he forced his leg up again, wishing it wasn't so hard. He was lucky to work remotely like this with anyone on his injury, he knew that, but it didn't stop him resenting the pain. Or how hard an exercise was that would have once been so simple for him to perform, and now left him sweating and cursing. The fact that his hand still hurt like hell from smashing it into a tree wasn't helping, either, although at least he could ice that for some instant relief.

A knock sounded out. Nate resisted the urge to get up and limp straight to the door.

"I'll let you off early to answer that."

"Thanks," Nate said, wiping the sweat from his face with an already damp towel. "But before I go, I wanted to ask you about talking to someone about some, er, some pretty dark night terrors I'm having. My counseling sessions have been pretty nonexistent lately."

The physio nodded. "Leave it to me, Nate. Someone will be in touch soon."

Nate felt the relief like a weight removed from his shoulders. "Thanks. Same time next week?"

"See you then. Keep up the good work."

Nate nodded and flipped the lid, ending the call. Another loud knock echoed out.

"Coming!" he called. Whoever it was they weren't the waiting type.

He didn't even consider that it could be Sarah. After the way he'd behaved yesterday? He doubted he'd be seeing her at all in the near future, if she had any control over it, and he wasn't exactly planning on seeking her out, either. Or at least not until he'd worked out an amazing apology to make up for what he'd said.

Nate pulled back the door, giving his face another wipe just in case it was…

"Holt," he said, seeing his brother standing on his doorstep.

"Hey, Nate."

There was a time when they'd never have had to knock on each other's doors, but now everything seemed strained. Completely unnatural when before everything they had done seemed like second nature, and Nate had no idea what to do about it.

"You, ah, want to come in?" Nate asked, not sure what else he was supposed to say.

"Nah, I've got a lot to do, but I promised Kathryn that I'd come over and ask you up for dinner tomorrow night." Holt stood with his hat in his hands, shifting his weight from foot to foot like he was as uncomfortable as hell. "I told her you'd probably say no, but…"

"I'll be there," Nate said, shaking off the desperate urge to tell Holt exactly what he'd expected to hear. Two family dinners within a few days would break some kind of a record for him, based on the past couple of weeks.

"You will?" Holt looked up and made eye contact with him, holding his gaze steady.

Nate stared back at his brother, wishing things didn't feel like this between them. He loved Holt, wanted to spend time with him and hang out like they used to. But nothing was the same anymore—nothing felt the same no matter how hard he wished it did. What he needed was to know Holt wasn't going to ask him for details, want to hear what had happened or why he wasn't the same man who'd left Larkville.

"I need some time alone, Holt. But it doesn't mean I don't want to see you guys." A knot formed low in Nate's throat, thick like he'd never dislodge it. But he needed to *try.* "Anyone else be there?"

Holt smiled, the grin starting slow and spreading across his face. "My wife likes a crowd, but if you'd rather it just be the three of us, that's fine by me."

Nate pushed his shoulders up, then down, hoping it looked like a casual shrug even though he was shaking on the inside at the thought of another family dinner. *The last one hadn't exactly gone as planned, and he'd as good as walked out on his sister the other night, even if it had been for an entirely different reason.* He still hadn't made it over to her place to apologize, either.

"You don't want to come out and give me a hand with a rogue bull, do you?" Holt asked. "I can ask someone else but as far as I recall you were pretty good with the big fellas."

Nate laughed, taken by surprise. Holt grinned

back at him, taking Nate way back in time, and it felt good.

"Let me get my boots on," he told his brother. "I was about to hit the shower but I might leave it till after."

"You might want to put some pants on, too. Those shorts make you look like a city boy."

Nate scowled back at Holt as he walked backward and flexed his muscles. "Watch it. I'll have you know I've been working out with the army doc."

Holt swallowed, hard enough for Nate to notice, and everything changed again—the easy banter ending like it had never existed. The unsaid things between them like a silent bubble that had risen to push them apart, Holt's eyes flickering back to Nate's leg, to his limp. Making it so obvious what he was thinking about.

I'm not the man I used to be. My leg will never be whole again, and neither will I.

"I'll be out in a sec," Nate said, biting his tongue against the words he was so close to snapping out, so close to telling his brother to screw the bull wrangling and spend the afternoon alone.

Holt looked uncomfortable again. "I'll wait outside."

Nate walked into his room and pulled a pair of jeans from the floor where he'd left them earlier. One minute he thought he'd made progress, that maybe there was a chance of things reverting back to almost normal again. And the next he came crashing back to reality, knowing that no matter what happened, he'd always be the outcast now.

He'd made choices that had changed his life forever, and he doubted anything would ever feel normal again, no matter what the future had in store for him. He'd loved his early years in the army, but now the one year that he'd hated seemed to tarnish everything in his life.

"You need to talk to someone, Jimmy. I can't cover for you any longer."

Jim inhaled the cigarette like his life depended

on it, and Nate recoiled from the sharp aroma. "I'm fine. I just need you to get off my back and leave me the hell alone."

"If you're not focused out there, one of us could die. I need you to be all there, Jimmy, please. One last op and they might look at letting us retire early, okay? We can go home, get out of here and start over. Take a job training recruits or something. Get back to loving what we do every day."

He watched his friend shake his head, still drawing back hard on the cigarette. Nate hadn't known when Jimmy had started smoking, but now he seemed to go through packet after packet.

"You don't need to worry about me, all right? If I'm not okay I'll do something about it myself."

Nate tugged a fresh T-shirt over his head and made for the door. It didn't matter where he was or who he was with, nothing could change what had happened to him. Because seeing Jimmy in his mind, reliving those conversations, the nightmares he had every night and the constant pain in his leg—they'd remind him of his past for the rest of his life.

He just knew it.

It was as if the bullet fragments left in his calf locked in memories that he would forever be powerless to forget.

Sarah's kitchen table was covered with papers and she had no idea where to start. Or she knew where to start, but her mind wasn't on the task.

She slumped down until her forehead met the cool of the wooden table and put her hands out palms down. *Her life was a disaster. A complete, utter disaster.* Everywhere she looked she seemed to see happy couples or pregnant women, like what she couldn't have was haunting her. Which was stupid, because she knew there were plenty of other options, even if she wanted to adopt or foster kids on her own one day.

And then there was Nate.

Argh. There had *always* been Nate, tucked away in the back of her mind if he wasn't right there at the front of it. Her marriage had ended because of plenty of things, but her not being able to fall pregnant had been a major reason. But if she was true to herself, she'd never felt for Todd what she'd felt for Nate. She'd always known it, but Todd was here and Nate had left her, and she'd tried to be a good wife to her husband, done everything within her power to make her marriage work.

But not being able to get pregnant hadn't been something she could control, and even though she'd slowly come to terms with it, her husband never had.

Her phone rang, its shrill noise making her jump and smack her knees on the table.

"Ouch!" She padded barefoot across the timber floor and reached for it. "Mom, I'm fine. Honestly," she said as she pressed the phone to her ear.

"Sarah?"

The deep, silky tone of the voice on the other end made her mouth go dry. *Walking-through-the-desert-all-day kind of dry.*

"Nate?" she asked, knowing full well that it was him on the other end. When he'd first left and she'd been under the illusion that he'd return, she'd held her breath waiting for the phone to ring. To hear that sexy-as-hell voice on the other end of the line. Now, his tone was an octave deeper, more a man now than the young guy who'd left back then. But it was undeniably *Nate.*

"Yeah, it's me," he said. She could hear the faint whisper of his breath as he paused and exhaled. She hadn't expected to hear from him at all.

"Are you okay?" she asked. Something must be wrong for him to be calling her.

"Can I come and see you, Sarah? Meet up with you somewhere?" he asked.

Sarah nodded before realizing that he couldn't see her. She didn't regret what she'd said to him yesterday, because it had been the truth, but they did need to clear the air between them properly. "Of course. Let's avoid town, though, shall we? I don't need the gossip mill firing into life over me again. Come to my place and we can have a coffee or something."

"I'll see you soon."

He hung up the phone and left Sarah with a shiver that patrolled its way up and down her spine, over and over again. She took a moment to collect her thoughts before walking calmly over to the desk and gathering up the papers she'd been shuffling.

She had plenty of time to organize the festival over the summer break, that wasn't the problem. But having Nate in her home? In the house she'd shared for so long with his friend? Now that was something she'd never be able to prepare for no matter how long she spent trying.

Maybe Nate was coming over to apologize, maybe it was something else entirely. What-ever the reason was behind his wanting to meet, though, she wanted her house to look present-able and she needed to have something to put out for him to eat.

Sarah glanced at her wristwatch. If he left the ranch soon it gave her less than fifteen or twenty minutes. Forget *the house*. If Nate was coming over, *she* wanted to look good. If her place was a little messy, then so be it.

She'd spent years wishing she could show Nate what he was missing, that she could make him remember what they'd had, to make him regret leaving her. Ending things the way they had. Because no matter how much he blamed her for becoming an item with his friend, he'd pushed her to it. If Nate hadn't left her, then she would have waited for him. *But a girl couldn't wait for-ever, and she hadn't.*

Nate had been the love of her life, but she'd wanted a family so badly, wanted to build a life here in the town she loved *with someone she loved*. The only problem was that she'd been missing one vital ingredient: Nate. Marrying Todd had been one of the biggest mistakes of her life.

CHAPTER EIGHT

NATE knocked at the door and stood back. He didn't really know what he was doing at Sarah's place or how he was going to apologize, but after the hour he'd spent in his brother's company he knew he had to do something.

Holt hadn't said or done anything wrong, but that was half the trouble. *It was what he wasn't saying, the questions in his gaze, the uncomfortableness between them, that was eating him up from the inside.* When all he wanted was to be around someone who treated him like there was nothing wrong.

He had no idea why, but Sarah was the only person he seemed able to tolerate right now, to be himself around, and yet he'd done a great job of trying to push her away already. When all she'd wanted to do was be there for him.

He stepped up to knock again just as the door was flung open.

"Hi!" A flushed-faced Sarah smiled at him from the doorway.

"Hey." Nate tried not to shake his head. He'd been brooding most of the afternoon and yet seeing Sarah had somehow made him want to smile again. Her hair was in a ponytail that was curling over her shoulder like she'd just been playing with it, her eyes bright even though he'd expected her to be angry. He would have forgiven her for still being wild with him.

"Come in," she told him, turning her back to lead the way. "Sorry about the mess but—"

Nate caught her wrist before she could take another step, forcing her to spin around. He kept the contact loose, his fingers curled around her soft skin, thumb stroking the base of her hand. "Sarah, I'm sorry," he said, not wanting to wait any longer when bringing up what had happened would be even more awkward. He needed to clear the air now while he still could.

Sarah didn't say anything. Her gaze was trained on his hand and Nate couldn't read her expression. Was she scared of his touch? Scared that he would physically hurt her again? *He hoped not.* And he certainly didn't want to hurt her with his words, either.

"I hope you know that I would never hurt you intentionally, Sarah." He took a deep breath, tried to find the right words, struggling to express how he was feeling. "What I said to you yesterday was rude and uncalled for, and I hate that I…"

She looked up when he stopped. "What?"

Nate squeezed her hand tight, then took a step back. "I hate that my dreams are so real, so vivid, that I don't even realize they *aren't* real. When I woke up and you were holding me, I freaked out. I thought I was back in Afghanistan, that you were the enemy, and instead all you were trying to do was help me. It's like I lose myself sometimes and it's hard coming back from that, but I am getting help for it. I promise."

Sarah's honesty was something he'd missed, something he'd craved since they'd been apart. She'd never been scared to say it like it was, to tell him when he was being an idiot or point him in the right direction. And he could tell that was exactly what she was about to do now.

"Nate, what you said before was the truth. I *did* take up with your friend, and it might have seemed fast to you because you were away, but I'd been on my own for almost two years. *Two years of not being with you.* So when we ended our relationship it was different for me than it was for you. It felt like it had been over for a long time when we finally called things off, and I was just so angry with you."

Nate swallowed. It was the truth, but it didn't make it any easier to hear. "Let's not go there," he suggested, hoping she'd agree. "Let our past stay in the past."

Sarah's smile was bittersweet. "I was hoping

the same thing, but you brought it up, Nate." She raised her shoulders in a modest shrug. "Now we've started I think we have to clear the air."

She was right. "Bourbon again?" he asked.

Sarah laughed, the moment of humor making her entire face ignite into a burst of happiness. "After the headache I woke up with? I think we'd best stick to coffee. And while we're apologizing, I'm sorry, too, Nate. I never should have slapped you."

"Forgiven," he told her. "And I probably deserved it, anyway."

Nate followed her into the kitchen and sat in the chair closest to the counter. He watched as Sarah moved gracefully to the refrigerator and back again, before pulling down two cups for their coffee.

"What?"

Nate stopped thrumming his fingers on the counter. He hadn't even realized he'd been doing it until Sarah had spoken. "Huh?"

"What's wrong? You're staring at me and playing my counter like it's an instrument."

He grimaced. "Old habit. Sorry."

Sarah set his cup in front of him and moved around to the other side of the table. She sat down, fingers dancing around the handle of her own cup before letting out a big sigh. "Nate, what are we even doing here?"

"You mean right now?" he asked, not sure where she was going with her sudden line of questioning.

"I mean now, today, yesterday." Sarah shook her head and blew on her coffee to cool it before looking up at him again. "Why are we even putting ourselves through this?"

He wished he knew. "I don't know, Sarah, but what I do know is that it's been nice seeing you again. Not that you'd know it, from the way I've been acting, but you're the first person I've seen in a long while who's…"

She held her cup dead still, midair, and stared at him. "Who's what?"

Nate swallowed a hot swig of coffee, grimacing as it burned his mouth and throat. "You've made me feel something again, Sarah, and I haven't experienced that in a long while." There, he'd said it. "Even if we get angry at each other, at least I was feeling *something*."

Sarah slowly put down her coffee. "I don't understand."

He didn't know how else he could explain it. "I'm not into talking about my feelings, Sarah, you know that."

She looked down. Nate could see the disappointment all over her face.

He shook his head. *What the hell was he even trying to achieve talking to her about all this?*

"I've been angry, happy, sad—all those things since I saw you the other day, and nothing has even made me *feel* in such a long time. I just want you to know that somehow you've helped me. That's all."

She met his gaze, a shy smile back in residence on her face. "I saw Todd yesterday."

"He's here?"

"Yup. With his pregnant girlfriend, too. We were supposed to meet yesterday evening but he's put it off until tomorrow. Thankfully he left a voice mail for me, so I didn't actually have to speak to him."

Now Nate was angry. *Real angry.* It wasn't his place, but… "Do you want me to teach him a lesson?" Just thinking about him breaking Sarah's heart was enough to fill him with rage. His hands balled into fists beneath the table, just like they had the other night when they'd spoken about his former friend. But showing his face around here with his girlfriend?

"No," Sarah told him, her eyes never leaving his. "I hate that I'm about to become a divorcée, but the truth is that I wasn't in love with Todd—I hadn't been in a long time. I was ready for a fresh start, so him leaving wasn't the worst thing that could have happened. It was how it happened that stung."

Nate's pulse started to race. He shouldn't care,

but hearing Sarah say that, telling him that she wasn't in love with her husband, was seriously affecting him. "So you're okay with seeing him back here?"

Sarah started playing with her ponytail, a sure sign that she either wasn't telling the truth or that she was struggling with…something that he couldn't figure out yet.

"It's not him, it's…" Her voice trailed off.

"What?" he asked.

Sarah sat back and started sipping at her coffee. "Nothing, forget I even said anything."

Nate was curious, but he wasn't going to pry. "You sure you don't want me to rough him up a little? Scare him perhaps?"

Sarah rolled her eyes. "Yeah, I want you to beat the guy up and end up in jail for assault. That would *really* help me out."

He held up his hands, pleased that they were at least having a civil conversation. After the way things had gone the day before, he'd have understood if she didn't speak to him at all, let alone sit in her kitchen joking around.

They sat in silence, both sipping their coffee. It didn't seem to matter that they weren't talking because it didn't feel strained, but he'd come here to ask for more than just her forgiveness.

"Sarah, when I told you that I'd help you out with Todd, if you needed me to pretend that we were something more, I wasn't joking."

Her cheeks flushed, stained such a pretty pink that he had to look away. He hadn't meant to embarrass her.

"You don't need to do that," she told him, looking out the window like there was something she was interested in outside.

"Sarah?" Nate resisted the urge to reach for her hand, but he at least got her attention enough to make her turn back. "The reason I'm offering is because I need your help, too."

That made her turn her body back toward him. "With what?"

Nate took a big breath, hoping he'd know how

to ask her in the right way. "I agreed on a full family dinner tonight, and the last one didn't exactly go well on my first night back," he admitted. "I was hoping that you'd come with me, just so, you know."

Sarah looked confused, but she collected their empty cups from the table and walked them into the kitchen instead of staying seated across from him. "Are you saying that you want us to pretend to be back together again, for real?"

Nate cringed. When she said it like that it didn't sound so great. "It would help me out if the heat was taken off me a bit, that's all. And I don't want to lie to anyone—I just want to take you with me. It'll be kind of like the other night, but with a few more Calhouns and me on better behavior."

She laughed as she put the cups into the dishwasher. "It sounds to me like this would put a *heap* of heat on you."

Maybe, but… "It would take the heat off them asking about what happened to me before I came home, and about my leg and…" He paused. "I wouldn't be asking you if it didn't mean a lot to me. You don't owe me anything, Sarah, but I'd really appreciate if you would come."

Sarah stopped moving then and stared at him, long and hard. "If I say yes, you'll have to agree to my terms, too."

Right now he would agree to anything if it meant her coming with him to dinner. "Shoot."

"I want you to promise that you'll tell *me* about what happened before you came home, when you're ready."

Nate shut his eyes, pushing the inferno of memories away, the ball of fire that was so hard to shut out. "That's not something I can promise," he told her, forcing his eyes to remain open, to ignore the thoughts starting to circle his mind like vultures.

"Well, you're going to have to if you want my help," she insisted, all businesslike, as if they'd been bartering nothing more than goods.

Nate stared at her, long and hard. Why did she want to know so bad?

Sarah smiled. "On second thought, perhaps you were right about Todd. If I'm going to help you out, then maybe I should take you with me when we meet tomorrow."

Sarah watched Nate and hoped she hadn't pushed him too far insisting that he talk to her about his injury, but she knew that if she didn't no one else would. His family had clearly gone about it in the wrong way, and she had no intention of making the same mistake twice where Nate was concerned.

She'd tried being passive, but he wanted her to do something for him and she had to use that leverage if she had a hope of actually helping him.

"Yes to the second condition."

Sarah took a step closer, planting both hands on the counter and leaning toward him. "Yes to both," she insisted. "This isn't a negotiation here, Nate, it's all or nothing."

Nate scowled at her. "You must drive the kids in your classroom mad."

She shook her head. "I want to be there for you, Nate, and I'm not going to force you, so at least say that you'll try to tell me about what happened. What you can, when you can."

He stood, his large frame seeming massive in her kitchen. The table was like a child's version with him standing beside it, his height and breadth making her want to back down. *Fast.*

"Fine," he snapped. "But if I do deck your idiot husband when I see him, you'll only have yourself to blame for making me so angry."

Sarah touched her hand to his arm as she walked past him again. She knew it must be hard for him to think about Todd, doubted they'd ever spoken again since she'd started a relationship with him.

"Do you wonder how things would have turned out, if I hadn't left?"

Nate's husky-voiced question took her by surprise. She spun around, slowly, wishing she was in the middle of doing something so she didn't have to stand so close to him and look into his eyes when she answered.

"Often." She didn't know what else to tell him. Did he want to know how much she'd craved him? How many times she'd wished the man lying in her bed beside her had been him? How badly she'd hoped he would change his mind and come back for her?

"Do you think we'd have lasted? That we'd be married with a brood of kids?" Nate asked.

Sarah stared into his eyes. Into eyes that still seemed to have a pathway straight to her heart, that made her want to throw her arms around him and whisper in his ear that everything would be okay. That they could go back in time and change what had happened.

But it wouldn't have mattered if Nate had stayed or not, because they would never have had the family they'd often talked about, that he'd wanted.

"I don't know, Nate, maybe," she lied. "But

let's not dwell on what could have been. It's not like you're never going to have the chance to marry a nice girl and have a family one day."

He chuckled. "You say it like it's a possibility for me and not for you."

Sarah did her best to keep the smile plastered on her face, to not let it waver. "I don't think that's what I want anymore, Nate," she lied.

She wasn't fooling him. "You were made to be a mom, we both know that."

Sarah bit her bottom lip to stop it from quivering, dug her nails into her palm. *This was not a conversation she was ready to have with anyone, let alone Nate Calhoun, the man she'd always dreamed of starting a family with.*

"Things change, Nate," she told him, willing her voice not to crack. "Sometimes we don't get what we want."

He stared at her, his eyes narrowing. He didn't believe her any more than she believed herself.

"So dinner tonight, right?" she asked, doing

her best impression of happy, as if his line of questioning hadn't bothered her at all.

Nate cleared his throat. "Yeah." He gave her another long, hard look before shaking his head slightly, like he was accepting that their conversation was at a close. "Want me to swing by and pick you up?"

She shook her head. "You don't need to come all the way out here to get me. How about we meet at your place?"

Nate brushed past her as he made for the door, and she had to stop herself from reaching out and pulling him back. Part of her was so desperate to go back in time, to rekindle something with Nate, but the realist part of her knew it would be a mistake.

He was a different man now, but he still deserved to be a dad. Even if they miraculously *could* rekindle what they'd had, it wouldn't work long term, and she couldn't bear her heart to be broken again. She'd already taken about all the heartache she could handle for a lifetime, and having to tell Nate that she was incapable of having a child, of their relationship slowly breaking down like her marriage had, wasn't something she could ever prepare herself for. Just because she was at peace with her infertility didn't mean he should have to be.

"I'll see you tonight, then," she said, leaning against the doorframe as he walked out onto her porch.

Nate turned, landing less than a foot or two away from her. She had to tilt her head back slightly to look up at him, to see his face, to watch the changing expressions there. He bent, so close, and Sarah shut her eyes. Lost herself in the faint scent of his cologne, of the feel of his body so near to hers.

Nate placed a featherlight kiss to her cheek, his lips hovering for longer than necessary, enough time for a shiver to trawl its way deliciously up and down her back, goose bumps tickling her skin.

"See you later," he said, voice low as he stepped away.

Sarah smiled, wrapping her arms around herself to stave away an imaginary coolness that was making her shiver. "Bye."

She watched as Nate walked through her front gate and around to the driver's side of his 4x4. His side profile was strong and masculine, his frame easily filling one side of the cab. He was so messed up from whatever had happened to him, far from the guy she'd known, but then he went and did something like that and made her realize that the Nate she'd once loved was still hiding in there. *Somewhere.*

Sarah smiled as he waved, hoping that he wouldn't notice the tears silently running down her face. She was powerless to stop them, unable to swallow away the emotion building with fury within her.

What had she done to deserve so much pain? Why had the man she loved so much left her, and then come home so damaged? Why was he finally home, finally within reach after so many years, and yet still so far away?

She shut the door, kicked off her shoes and made her way to the bathroom. Just because she was feeling sorry for herself didn't mean she wasn't going to look good. Being by Nate's side again, around his family, might be bittersweet but it wasn't exactly going to be difficult. She'd spent years around the table in the big ranch house, been part of their family on more occasions than she could ever count.

She'd loved Nate with all her heart once, and if she was honest with herself she doubted she'd ever stopped.

CHAPTER NINE

NATE was exhausted. Bone-achingly, mind-shat-teringly exhausted. He let his head drop into his hands, fighting the fatigue that he battled on a daily basis. Why wouldn't his mind just shut off? He couldn't stop thinking about Sarah wanting him to talk, but if it was this bad inside of his own head, how would he ever cope with telling the truth? With speaking it out loud?

He ran his hands through his hair—hair that was still shorter than he'd once worn it. Back when he'd lived on the ranch, before he'd joined the army, his brother had always made fun of him, called him Goldilocks. *It seemed like a lifetime ago.*

A knock made him rise, shaking him back into action. *If only he could sleep, could actually fall into a deep slumber for an entire night and not be thrown back into the world he was trying so desperately to escape from, maybe he wouldn't feel like such a zombie.*

Right now, though, he had to pull himself together and deal with seeing all his family again for dinner, and figure out what the hell was eating Sarah up so bad. It was more than just Todd, he could sense it. Her idiot husband had sure caused her some definite heartache, but she was upset over something deeper than just her marriage failing.

Wow.

"You look amazing." Nate didn't even try to disguise it as he looked Sarah up, then down. She was more beautiful now than the day he'd first met her—there was a maturity to her face, to the way she held herself, that made her even more striking.

"You don't look so bad yourself," she said to him. Nate could see the blush creeping over her cheeks, though, knew that she was struggling with his compliment.

"I don't really think my jeans and shirt put me in the same league as you, but thanks."

She was wearing a dress, cut low enough on her chest to make his mind race in a different direction, but brushing the tops of her knees to make it more demure than he'd have preferred. Still, he more than liked it.

"Is it too much?" Sarah asked, her eyes flashing with what he guessed was concern.

Nate chuckled, forcing himself to look off into the distance for a split second, to stop thinking about how enticing the woman standing at his door was. *How jaw-droppingly beautiful Sarah was.* "Sarah, you look great. Maybe it's just because I've been around men for so long, but I'd forgotten how…" He paused, not wanting to embarrass her or say the wrong thing. "You're beautiful, Sarah, absolutely beautiful."

She stared at him before punching his shoulder softly. "Nate," she groaned.

He grabbed her hand before she could with-draw it, his reflexes fast. His fingers curled tight around her wrist, holding it against him, her knuckles still brushing his right shoulder.

Nate knew he shouldn't have done it, that he should have just laughed and let her hit him, let her treat him like a brother or friend with her play punch, but damn it, he had no interest in being a friend to her.

Right now, he wanted more. A lot more.

"Nate?" Her voice was a low whisper, but she didn't move. Didn't struggle or try to pull her hand from his viselike grip.

He didn't know what to say to her, but he knew what he wanted to do.

Nate tugged her in closer, not letting go of her, forcing Sarah to pull up against his chest. She didn't resist, but he could tell she wasn't sure, either. Wasn't sure what he was about to do, and he had no intention of keeping her guessing.

Nate slowly moved her hand down, away from his shoulder, running his other arm up her body, caressing the small of her back with his fingers. She was a perfect fit against him, her shallow breathing only spurring him on.

He bent, inch by inch, until her chin tilted. Until her lips parted, inviting him, and he didn't hesitate.

Nate crushed her mouth to his, no longer gentle, needing to have Sarah against him, needing to feel her body tight to his. He fought against the urge to fist his hand in her hair, forcing himself to cup the back of her skull instead, to kiss her like he'd imagined kissing her all those lonely nights when he'd been on his own on the other side of the world. When he'd wished he'd been selfish enough to ask her to wait for him, so he could forge on with his career and know the woman he loved was still waiting for him back home. But asking her to keep waiting for years wouldn't have been fair, and he'd loved her enough to want to set her free.

Sarah's low moan brought him back to reality,

made him pull his lips away from her, to take a breath and think about what he'd just done.

But Sarah had other ideas.

Nate found himself staggering backward as Sarah placed a hand flat to his chest, pushing him backward with a force he hadn't even imagined she possessed. Pain flashed through his leg as he took one more step, before finding his back pressed hard to a wall.

Sarah's hand was still holding him in place, but she never said anything. Instead, she reached up fast, her fingers twisting into his short hair, tugging him down, forcing his mouth to hers again.

And he had no reason to resist.

Sarah kissed him with a desperation that empowered him, that made him kiss her back with the same sense of recklessness, like they needed each other because their lives depended on it.

Until she removed her lips from his as suddenly as she'd kissed him, taking a step away and letting her hand trail away from him.

"Sarah?" His voice didn't even sound like his own, was deeper and confused.

She smiled and blushed beet-red. "I just need a minute to freshen up."

Then she walked away.

Nate laughed. He laughed like he hadn't laughed since he was a kid, tears falling down his cheeks as he stood alone, waiting for Sarah, wondering if he'd just imagined the fact that he'd been pressed against a wall in his own home and kissed in a way that had him desperate to call off dinner and take up where they'd finished off.

He had no idea where that kiss had come from, but he sure as hell wasn't complaining.

Sarah knew she was still blushing. Her embarrassment ran so deep that she was hot all over, and she could hardly bring herself to look at Nate. When she emerged from his bathroom, lipstick firmly back in place, they'd started walking up to the main house, but they hadn't said a word.

"Sarah, um…"

Until now.

"Please, Nate," she insisted, cringing inwardly as she kept her gaze trained ahead. "I don't know what happened before, so I think we should just forget about it." She was starting to wish a hole would open up and swallow her.

He chuckled. Nate was making fun of her! Right now she'd prefer quiet and brooding.

"It's kind of imprinted into my brain," he admitted.

When she didn't so much as look at him he caught her hand, swinging her around and forcing her to stop. "Sarah, it's not like we've never made out before."

She nodded, squirming on the stop as he watched her. *Not like that.*

"Sarah?"

Since when was he the chatty one? "I don't know what happened back there, Nate, but can we please not talk about it?"

He let go of her and raised both hands. "Fine

by me. I'm just saying that we shouldn't be all weird about—" he paused "—kissing."

Sarah groaned and started walking again. This was going to be an uncomfortable night, and not because she regretted what had happened between them. Kissing Nate had opened her eyes, made her realize what she'd been missing out on all these years, shown her why she and Todd had never been right for each other. Because Nate's lips against hers had made her body tingle like a fire had been stirred to life in her belly, made her remember what it had been like when they were together.

But it had also shown her what she would never have.

Nate took Sarah's hand as they walked in the door. He'd hesitated, about to knock, then realized that it was about time he started acting like he was home rather than a stranger on the ranch.

"You did tell them I was coming, right?" Sarah asked him as she gripped his hand.

Nate quickened his pace to get inside, so she wouldn't be able to explode once he told her the truth. "Not exactly. I figured surprising everyone would provide a good diversion."

"By letting me take all the heat?" she murmured.

Nate tugged her into the kitchen, and almost instantly wished he hadn't.

Four faces turned their way, and they each held a different expression. Johnny smiled, like he didn't realize what the big deal was. Jess shook her head slightly and grinned, like she knew something that no one else in the room did. Kathryn was shocked enough to see him hand in hand with Sarah that she stopped whatever she'd been doing at the counter, and Holt… Nate could have laughed at the expression on his brother's face. When they'd been kids, he'd never been able to surprise his brother or do anything to shock him, anything that Holt hadn't already done. But tonight? Holt was still holding his beer in the air like his arm had frozen before he'd been able to bring it to his lips.

Maybe holding Sarah's hand had been too much. Arriving with a date might have been shock value enough.

"I hope we're not late," Nate said, unsure what else to say to announce their presence, to put an end to the empty silence in the room.

No one said anything for a moment and Nate felt Sarah's hand slide away from his. *Damn.* He'd definitely gone about this in the wrong way.

"Nate, I'm so happy you decided to join us," Kathryn said, breaking the silence and giving her husband a noticeable kick on her way toward him. The imaginary weight dragging Nate's shoulders down was lifted as his brother ignored her and took a swig of beer instead. Kathryn reached them and leaned forward to kiss his cheek before touching Sarah's shoulder. "You, too, Sarah. So long as no one wakes Izzy up, I'm sure we'll have a relaxing evening."

He watched Sarah nod, but she was flustered.

"I was just telling Nate off for not warning you he was bringing someone."

Kathryn shrugged like they hadn't all received the shock of their lives when he'd arrived with a woman. "Don't be silly. We have plenty of food and a massive table. And besides, we're just pleased to have everyone together, right? The baby is down, the food's almost ready, and the company's great."

Kathryn turned to look at Holt, who seemed to realize he was expected to do or say something. "Yeah, it's, ah, good to see you both."

"Sarah, that horse of yours is looking good. I did some more work with her today," Johnny called out.

He watched as Sarah seemed to relax, leaving his side to head toward Johnny and Jess. Nate looked away from her to see his brother watching him, like he didn't know what to say.

"Beer?" Holt asked.

Exactly what they needed to settle things between them, shooting the breeze over a beer. "Sounds good."

He made his way over to where his brother had been seated and took the beer he offered when he returned. "Thanks for asking me over," Nate told him, knowing he was going to have to make an effort.

"Glad you could make it."

Nate didn't want to talk about Sarah after the conversation he'd had with Holt that first day he'd seen her again, but he knew he had to say something. "I should have called ahead and mentioned I was bringing someone."

Holt laughed. "I don't know if I'd call Sarah just *someone*."

Nate took another sip of beer, not sure what to say. It had been a long time since he'd just chatted like this and it was no longer something that came easy to him, especially with his brother. "It's been nice seeing her again." And he had to learn to open up, at least a little.

"You two were always good together. Made some of us wonder why you'd up and leave…."

"Don't go there." Nate hated the bite to his words but it was a knee-jerk reaction—he couldn't help it. "There are plenty of things I wish I hadn't done, Holt, and leaving here like that is one of them. I didn't exactly manage to achieve the right balance."

They sat in silence, staring at each other. Nate stood. "Maybe this wasn't such a good idea."

Holt stood, too, but he didn't look angry. He held out a hand instead, and when Nate didn't clasp it he grabbed hold of his upper arm, looked him straight in the eye. "Nate, I know I seem to keep saying the wrong thing, but don't walk away from us."

Nate stayed still, eye to eye with his brother. He knew the rest of the room had gone silent and he wished they were having this conversation in private. "There are things I can't talk about, Holt, and I need you to respect that." He was trying to stay calm but it didn't come naturally to him anymore.

Holt nodded and let go of his arm. "I don't want to be the enemy here, Nate. The truth is we're all pleased to have you back, even if things are a bit rough at the moment."

Nate shut his eyes, forced his anger away and held out his hand to Holt. His brother clasped it straightaway, holding on tight as they kept the grip for longer than they should have.

"You need to understand that I need time, Holt. I'm not, things aren't…nothing's the same for me right now."

Holt let go of him and sat back down. Nate did the same.

"Whatever you need, Nate, I'm here for you. Don't you forget it."

A hand on his shoulder made Nate jump, but he willed himself not to overreact. He was in his brother's home, not on some foreign battlefield. The conversation he'd had with the army counselor played back through his mind, the sense of calm he'd felt after talking to him on the phone earlier in the day.

"Hey." Sarah's warm, soft voice made him relax.

Nate touched her hand, let his fingers settle over her skin. *He was glad she was here, that he had her with him tonight.*

"You want to sit down?" Nate wished he could go back in time, was still close enough to Sarah that he could pull her around and down onto his knee. That she would happily sit on his lap and lean back into him.

More thoughts, more feelings, that he needed to suppress.

Sarah touched the back of his neck before walking off toward Kathryn. "I'm good," she said, but the look she gave him told him something else entirely. *She was nervous and he'd done little to help her fit back into his family's fold.* Everyone had always loved Sarah, but she was here for him and that meant he needed to make an effort where she was concerned, too.

It wasn't all about him and he needed to remember it.

Nate watched as Jess followed close behind Sarah. Johnny was hanging out with Brady in the adjoining room.

"I think I'll join the girls for a drink," Nate said, suddenly not able to take his eyes off Sarah, the one person in the world he'd come close to opening up to, and who he'd treated like crap these past few days. And yet she was still there for him, pretending their relationship was something more just to help him out.

Well, maybe they shouldn't be pretending.

"After you." Holt gave Nate a wink, like he'd known what he was thinking, or at least that he knew he'd been thinking about Sarah.

Sarah looked up, too, like *she* knew he was thinking about her, as well, but instead of the knowing look his brother had given him, Sarah's was shy. *Did she want this to be real, too, or was she just really good at make-believe?*

There was only one way to find out, and Nate

wasn't going to waste time figuring that out. He spent enough time already inside his own head, thinking about things that he couldn't control, that he couldn't go back in time and fix, but this was different. *This he could do something about.*

Sarah tried to focus on what Kathryn was saying to her, but she was having a hard time remembering what their conversation was even about. When she'd looked at Nate before, she'd been worried he was about to walk out and that things were about to become difficult, but now it was him watching her and she couldn't ignore it.

She looked across at him. Now he wasn't just looking at her, he was headed in her direction.

"Hey," he said, snaking his arm around her waist. "You okay?"

Sarah tried not to tense up but it didn't come naturally. Having Nate so close, his body so warm and… She took a slow, deep breath. "I'm good. Thanks." *Was he playing pretend still or was something else going on?* Regardless of what was going on between *them,* he looked happier than she'd seen him since he'd been back. More relaxed, and clearly getting on better with his family.

She glanced sideways at him, tried to ignore his arm still around her waist, loosely tucked behind her back like it belonged there. Part of her wanted to snuggle closer, but the other part of her, the sensible side that remembered how much it had hurt when he'd left her, told her to steer clear. Friendship, sure, but nothing more.

No matter how good his kisses were.

"Do you need a hand there, Kathryn?" she asked.

"Sure. How about you carry this to the table for me?" the other woman suggested. Sarah nodded and sidestepped away from Nate. She took the large serving dish and crossed the room, placing it on the middle of the table.

"Oh."

"I didn't mean to scare you."

Nate was standing behind her when she spun around.

"Is something wrong?" she asked, struggling to meet his gaze. Something had changed, something that she couldn't quite figure out.

"I just wanted to say thank-you for coming with me tonight. If you hadn't agreed to join me, I don't know if I'd have come at all, and you were right."

She tilted her head slightly, looking up at him. She forgot sometimes how tall Nate was. "About what?" she asked.

He held out a hand and she looked at it, paused before tucking her palm against his. There was something unnatural about touching him, about pretending, but there was also something comforting, too.

"You said I needed to give my family a chance, and you were right. It was never going to be easy, on them or me, but I need to try. Otherwise where am I ever going to belong?" Nate clasped her hand more tightly and used their interlocked fingers to draw her closer. His other hand rose to her face, cupping her cheek.

Sarah resisted the urge to close her eyes and lean into his touch. She couldn't go there. Anything that happened with Nate couldn't be permanent, couldn't be what they'd both once wanted, but would it be so bad to give in to her feelings *just for now?* "Nate, this doesn't feel like pretending anymore," she whispered.

His grin was lopsided when he smiled at her, his head moving slowly from side to side. "Maybe we're not."

Sarah took a quick step back when a throat was cleared, loudly, behind Nate.

"Sorry to interrupt but…" The sound of Holt's voice made her groan, but Nate didn't let go of her hand, not until she looked up at him, until their eyes met one last time.

"Of course," she said, in the bravest voice she could manage. "Dinner smells delicious."

Sarah kept her head down as she walked around to the other side of the table, hoping that

Nate wouldn't follow her. Everyone sat down and Brady took the heat off her and Nate with his chatter as he play-fought with Holt for the head-of-the-table seat.

But the heat never left Nate's gaze—she could sense him even without looking at him. Something had changed, *the game had a whole new set of rules that she didn't know about,* and the thought terrified her.

"Sarah, how's the festival coming along?" Kathryn asked as she took her seat.

"Are you offering to help?" Sarah quipped, pleased to have something to focus on other than Nate, even if it was just for a moment.

Everyone laughed, leaving Kathryn looking slightly bewildered.

"It's okay," Sarah told her. "They're just thinking about how much they *all* want to help me, right?" She made the mistake of looking at Nate then, while everyone else erupted into chatter about the festival. His smile spread slowly across his face as she watched him, his eyes finally sparkling like she'd remembered, the way they'd looked at her for so many years when they'd been in love.

"Thank you," he mouthed, gesturing with his head toward his brother and sister.

It *was* nice, being around the Calhoun family, being seated at a table and surrounded by happy people who loved one another. She'd be a liar if she didn't admit to still loving this family, and Nate, too, but it only made her fate more bitter-sweet. Her own table would never be surrounded by a brood of their children and their partners, if they did let something happen between them again. Because she might have come to terms with not being a biological parent one day, but it didn't mean Nate should have to make that compromise.

And there was nothing she could do about it. Not a thing.

Nate slapped his brother on the back, dropping a kiss to his sister's head as he passed, and to Kathryn's cheek, too.

"Thanks for having us," he said, taking Sarah's hand and leading her out onto the porch.

"It was lovely, thanks," Sarah called out, holding up her hand in a wave as they walked away.

"Nice to see you two lovebirds." Holt's laughter rang out behind them as they walked.

Nate shook his head and slung his arm around Sarah's shoulders, giving her a squeeze. "Kind of weird stepping back in time like that."

She sighed. "You can say that again."

They kept walking in the dark, side by side but not saying anything.

"Sarah, what I said before about not pretending…"

She stopped and looked up at him. "What are we doing, Nate?"

It was him sighing now, putting both his arms around Sarah's waist. "I don't know if I can answer that, but you know what?" He looked up at the sky, then back down at her. "All I know is that being back home was hard, *really hard,* until I saw you again. And somehow you've helped me to pull everything together."

She stepped toward him and placed her cheek against his chest, arms looped around his waist. "We can't just go back in time, Nate. Things have changed, *I've changed,* and you have a heap of stuff to work through."

Nate turned her in his arms so her back was pressed to his chest instead, tilted her back slightly to point up at the sky. "You see those stars up there?"

She nodded against him.

"I don't know anything about the constellations, but what I do know is that for years I stared up at the stars in whatever hellhole I was posted to, and I thought of you. You were always with me, even when I was so pissed with you for taking up with Todd, even though I knew deep down that I didn't have a right to be."

She stayed silent, warm against him, and he wrapped his arms around her tight.

"There's so much we need to say, so many things that we need to talk about, Nate."

He let her go when she pulled away, but she didn't go far.

"Like what?" Was there something going on with her that she needed to tell him? "What's wrong, Sarah?"

She reached out for him and placed her palm against his. "Being with your family tonight was a great first step, but you need to talk to someone about what you've been through. About—"

"Is this about what happened when I grabbed you? Sarah, you have to know that I would never hurt you. I know I scared you but, hell." He ran a hand through his hair, losing contact with her to do so. "I wish I could take it back. Both times. And I've already had my first counseling session."

"That's great, Nate. Because you need to deal with what's going on with *you,* get yourself in the right headspace, before we can even think about something happening with us."

Nate started to walk again, needing to move, and Sarah followed. She was right, Sarah always seemed to be right, but that didn't make her words any easier to digest.

"Do you know that Holt could hardly look me in the eye after I saw him looking at my leg earlier today?" he asked Sarah. "It was like a great white elephant was suddenly in the room with us, and I didn't know how to talk to him. Whether to make a joke or tell him to buzz off."

Sarah would have noticed he was limping, that there was no way he could walk this far or at this pace without it being obvious, but it was like she didn't even see it. Or maybe she just honestly didn't see it as a big deal.

"That's what I'm talking about, Nate," she said.

They reached his house and he unlocked the door, opening it for her to walk through. "Some things are better left unsaid," he told her.

"You can talk to me, Nate," Sarah told him, standing behind him when he whirled around. "I didn't mean to ruin our evening, but you need to talk, Nate, and I'm here to listen. About anything and everything, or just what you're prepared to tell."

CHAPTER TEN

NATE didn't know what was worse, the fact that Sarah seemed not to see his injury when everyone else seemed to notice it constantly, or that she had no problem asking him outright about what he'd been through.

His family had only seemed to feel sorry for him, wanted to know why he wasn't the same person who'd left when they'd asked him questions. Sarah? She wanted to know what he'd experienced, what had happened…the truth behind his experiences rather than just the end result.

"I don't think you understand what you're asking," he said, trying not to be angry with her, to acknowledge how strong and brave she was being.

Sarah's eyes looked like they were glowing,

but on second look he wondered if they were tears making her usual amber gaze appear so different.

"Nate, you have to talk to someone about more than just your night terrors. It doesn't have to be me, but if you want to fit in here again? If you want to be part of your family again and live the kind of life that I know you want, then you can't keep it all bottled up inside."

He wanted so badly to walk away, to tell himself that Sarah didn't know what she was talking about, but it was impossible. Because she meant something to him, and no matter how angry he became or how much she got under his skin, that wasn't going to change. And tonight he felt different. Something *had* changed between them, or maybe it was just something within him that had changed, but one thing he did know was that he didn't want to hurt her. Not again.

"Unless you've been where I've been, seen what I've seen, there's no way you can understand." Nate kept his voice as low as he could, controlling the pain and anger that surged within him whenever he spoke about his past. About his last year in Black Ops, what he'd been witness to, what he'd lost.

Sarah shook her head and leaned toward him. "I don't need to understand, Nate, but you do need someone to talk to." Sarah pressed her palm to his cheek, her eyes now obviously glistening with unshed tears—tears that he could only guess were for him. "What's it going to cost you to try me?"

Nate stood and walked away, paced to the door before whirling back and glaring at the woman looking up at him so expectantly. Giving him a chance to open up, even though he was so angry with her right now for asking him to do something he found so hard. But he didn't want to be that guy, the one freaking out whenever someone tried to talk to him about what he'd seen.

"Everything, Sarah," he choked out. "It already feels like it's cost me everything, what I went through."

Nate watched as she swallowed.

He ran as fast as he could, taking down the machine gun nest as he covered the ground. Jimmy was crumpled, collapsed, lying unprotected as round after round echoed out around them.

"I lied for someone I cared about, okay? Are you happy now that you've heard the truth?" The words snapped out of him, even though he didn't want them to. But talking about Jimmy, about what he'd witnessed, wasn't something he'd ever planned on sharing.

Sarah shook her head, her mouth hovering into a frown. "I'm happy that you're finally talking again, and that you're telling *me* the truth."

"I've never lied to you, Sarah. Never," he told her, wishing he could keep his anger in check but failing miserably now. "But reliving the past isn't going to help me!"

This time it was Sarah glaring at him. "Never lied to me? How about when you promised that you'd come home, that I was as important to you as the army was? How about when I waited for you, put my life on hold for you, and *you never came back?* I was so proud of you, Nate, of what you were doing, but I hadn't expected it to cost us our relationship."

He wanted to turn away from the tears he could see only barely restrained by her lashes, but he couldn't pull his eyes away from her face. "I said I'd never lied to you, not that I'd never broken a promise to you." Damn it, he knew he'd hurt her and what he'd done was wrong. He should never have left, never have ended things with her.

She laughed. "Oh, *I'm sorry.* I didn't realize there was any difference between the two."

It was something he'd never forgive himself for, and never stop regretting.

Nate cleared his throat, wishing he could walk away from a fight they were long overdue to have, but one that he'd hoped he'd manage to avoid. "When I told you what you meant to me, I wasn't lying, Sarah. Deep down, I know you believe that." He paused, not sure how to tell her what had happened, why things hadn't worked out the way they should have. "I never wanted to work on the land and I didn't want to give up doing what I loved, but when I joined up I hadn't realized how hard it would be fulfilling my dreams and feeling guilty about leaving you behind."

"If I'd known I was holding you back I would have finished our relationship myself." Her words were almost cruel, angry. "And don't give me that crap about not wanting to work the land, because you had a dream once, Nate. A dream you shared with me, and that was you serving our country and then coming back. Don't you remember? You wanted to spend time away, then come back and find a way to make a living here on the ranch, and then start a family here with *me*."

"I remember, Sarah. I will always remember," he said, reaching for her hands. "But you were brave enough to let me go, and I'll always admire you for that. It was just that, I don't even know how to explain this, but…" How had they ended up going back this far into the past, into what had happened between them, when only moments before he'd been starting to tell her about Jimmy? His plan had changed, what he wanted had changed, but the way he felt about her never had.

Sarah waited instead of pushing him away and Nate knew he had to continue. That if he didn't speak now she *would* walk away and he might never have the chance again.

"When I was offered the chance to become part of a special forces team, I would have been a fool not to accept. Or at least that's what I thought at the time. I was so young and it was something I'd dreamed of since I was a school-boy."

"So why are you back here, then?" she asked. "Tell me what brought you home, Nate. *Tell me.*"

Nate gripped her hands tighter, needing all of her strength as well as his to be honest with her about what had happened. He wasn't angry anymore, but talking was never going to come easy to him, not with his friend and the army as the subject matter.

"When I heard about you and Todd, I thought it was a sign that being Black Ops was what I was meant to be doing. Part of me had hoped you'd still wait, but it was stupid to even think that, when I told you it was over. But within a couple of years, I wanted out. Jimmy did, too, and we both tried. He was struggling and I didn't want to end up the same way. I knew something wasn't right with him, and not saying something, not interfering when I could have, cost him his life." Nate shook his head. "I went from loving my job more than anything to hating it."

Sarah was nodding and squeezing his hands in return. "Why did you want out?" Her anger had turned into concern.

Nate sighed. Talking wasn't getting any easier, but Sarah was there for him and he had to try. There were things he could tell her, because of what they'd shared in the past, that he knew he'd never be able to divulge to anyone else. Not even his family.

"Because it didn't feel right. And because..." Nate gulped and watched as Sarah did the same. "Because after losing you, and then Mom passing away, I realized that I'd left the place I actually belonged. I'd been searching all this time, wanting to serve my country and prove myself on my own, and at the same time I'd managed to lose everything that was important to me. I might not have realized it straightaway, but hand on my heart it's the truth. All I wanted was to come back here, but now that I'm here it's like I no longer fit in anywhere."

Sarah looked numb, like she was in shock and didn't know how to respond. "Then when Dad passed away and my friend, too, it was like everything had been taken away from me. Like I had nothing left." He looked up and into Sarah's beautiful, amber-gold eyes. "Until I saw you again."

Sarah's cheeks turned the softest shade of pink as she smiled. "You don't need to say that, Nate. Flattery won't get you anywhere with me."

He stroked her face from the edge of her eye to the curve of her mouth, then cupped her chin. "*But it's the truth.* I came home a broken man, and when I thought I was beyond repair, somehow you managed to save me."

"What happened out there, Nate? What happened to your friend?"

Nate's body shuddered like a bolt of lightning had hit it. No one else in the world knew what had happened out there that day, no one but him. *And the friend he'd watched kill himself.*

"You have to realize that when I joined the special forces, when I became part of one of the most elite military operations in the world, I pledged to keep what I saw, where I was and what I did a secret." Nate sucked in a big breath. "What happened on tour had to stay on tour, no question about it."

Sarah tucked her arms around his torso and

hugged him tight. "But something happened over there, Nate. Something that you need to talk about before the secrecy of it eats you alive." She paused. "This isn't me asking because I'm nosy, this is me asking because I want to help. And if it's not me you talk to, then it has to be someone else, and soon."

Nate had no idea how she could be so compassionate toward him when he'd already hurt her so bad, when only moments before they'd been arguing.

Jimmy's lifeless, heavy body weighed him down so much he could hardly walk. The pain in his own leg was so intense that Nate thought it might have been on fire. That it had somehow been set alight.

He was yelling, over and over, screaming for someone to help Jimmy.

And knowing that no matter what happened, he was never going to be able to tell the truth. Not to anyone.

Except Sarah. Right now.

"Once I tell you, I need you to not ask me about it ever again. But I need to know that you're sure?"

"Sure that I can keep it a secret or sure that I want to know?"

Nate held her hand, pleased that for once he wasn't trying to fight having her near. "I already know I can trust you with a secret, Sarah. What I need to know is whether you want the burden of knowing what happened to me that day."

Sarah smiled at him, honesty shining from her eyes with an unmistakable glow. "Tell me, Nate. When I said I was here for you it wasn't an empty promise. I don't say anything I don't mean."

Nate pulled her hard against him in a fierce embrace before letting go so he could face her. They sat on the sofa, Nate staring into Sarah's eyes.

"When I said before that Jimmy was struggling, *he was really struggling.* He had been my best friend for years, and I knew him as well as anyone in my life. There were days near the end that I had to cover for him constantly, because I knew he wasn't capable of doing what was required of him, what was expected of us. And I knew he was getting worse. We'd served together before Black Ops, so I knew something was wrong because we were so close we may as well have been brothers."

Sarah nodded, encouraging him to continue.

It was a fight to expel the words. They were in his mind but stuck in his throat before he could tell her what he suddenly wanted to share so bad it hurt. Like a knife being twisted in his chest.

"I knew things were bad, but I couldn't bring myself to do anything about it. He kept insisting he was fine, or he wouldn't talk about it at all, and if I'd said something to our superior then, I knew he'd be out. And what would that have meant for the rest of his life? For his wife waiting at home? What would a dishonorable discharge have meant for him?"

"And now you think you did the wrong thing

in not saying something?" Sarah asked, her voice soft and full of concern.

"I don't think, Sarah, *I know.*" Nate tried hard not to let himself be sucked back into the world he was trying so hard to pull away from—the world of memories that never seemed to stop hunting him out. "The official records tell of enemy fire taking out my best friend. About me being injured when our operation went bad. I've never told anyone that I watched as Jim turned his gun on himself and took his own life, or that I was shot because I ran as fast as I could to save him, firing at two separate machine gun nests, and got shot in the process. But that's the truth of it, Sarah. Because I didn't speak up and do the right thing, I cost my friend his life."

Nate was suddenly gulping for air, fighting to breathe. His body began to convulse, before a massive sob erupted from his chest.

"Nate, oh, Nate. Come here." Sarah grabbed him tight and tucked his head to her chest, cradling him like she would one of her young pupils.

"I'm sorry, I…" Nate couldn't even talk, he was crying so damn hard and he couldn't stop it. *He was crying like a baby in front of the one woman in the world that he wanted to be strong for.*

"There's no shame in crying, Nate. I'm here for you, I'm here," she whispered, her lips close to his ear.

She was right. *Sarah wasn't the girl he needed to impress; she was the one he could be himself with.*

Somehow her words pulled his emotions back in check. He took a deep, shuddering breath and reached for her face, cupping her cheeks gently in between both his hands. "I love you, Sarah."

Tears sprang into her eyes then. "Nate, you don't need to say that," she mumbled.

He didn't let go of her face even when she tried to look away, to force his gaze from her.

"So all of a sudden you don't want me to be honest with you?"

Her bottom lip had started to quiver. "You mean it, don't you?" she whispered.

"I only say what I mean, Sarah," he told her, bringing his face closer to hers. "I'd rather stay silent than lie, and you're still the only woman I've ever said *I love you* to."

That got her attention. He could see the question in her eyes, the disbelief, but it was true.

"Are you sure?" she asked, a shy smile kicking up the edge of her lips.

"It's not the sort of thing I'd forget," he told her, trying not to laugh. "*I love you, Sarah.* Always have, probably always will. Hand on my heart, you're the only woman I've ever told, aside from my mom and my sister."

She shook her head, her bottom lip caught between her top teeth as she watched him. Nate took his chance. Talking to her had helped, had felt right, but he knew what would make him feel a whole heap better.

Kissing Sarah again.

Nate knelt and tugged Sarah from the sofa, pulling her down to his level. She obeyed, her eyes trained on his, not resisting when he pressed his lips to her throat, pushing away her hair with one hand and holding her close with the other.

"Nate?"

He trailed more kisses down her collarbone. "Mmm?"

"Are you sure this is a good idea?"

He chose not to answer with words. Nate cupped Sarah's face with both hands, eyes focused on her full lips. They parted when he kissed her, her body softening against his, hands snaking around his hips.

But it didn't last for long.

Sarah's confidence seemed to have grown. She was no longer blushing but smiling at him when she pushed him away like she was a woman in charge of her own destiny. *And right now he hoped that immediate destiny included him.*

Nate groaned as Sarah placed her palm to his

chest. *Last time she'd taken charge he hadn't exactly minded, and her plans this time didn't disappoint him.*

She slowly pushed him, more gentle than she'd been earlier, but her message was clear. Nate grimaced as his leg bent in an uncomfortable position.

"Are you okay?" She stopped moving, her hand fluttering away from him.

"Fine," he growled, grabbing her hand and placing it back flat to his chest. Nate lay back, trying hard not to take over and lay claim on Sarah with his hands, pulling her down on top of him instead.

But Sarah was setting the pace, and he wanted to let her, wanted her to decide what she was comfortable with.

She sat astride him and Nate didn't fight it, even though he wasn't used to anyone else taking charge of anything in his life. He'd resisted contact with anyone for so long, jumped when he was touched, needed to be in charge. *Until now.* Because Sarah wasn't going to hurt him, wasn't doing anything other than be there for him, and he was ready to at least try to trust again. "You're gonna have to go slow with me," he joked, pulling her farther down onto him. Her hair fell over the sides of his face, tickling his throat.

"This slow?" she joked, giggling as she pressed tiny kisses across his jaw.

"Just hurry up and kiss me, woman," he growled, flipping her over so she was trapped beneath him, his patience long expired.

Sarah loved the indent of Nate's body above her, the weight of his large frame. She could do this. How long had she thought about Nate? Remembered the way things had been between them?

It didn't matter what couldn't be, it was about *right now.* Being loved, even just for one night, by Nate. Even if she had made him tell her everything without sharing her own fears, her own secrets, that she was terrified of confessing to him. Even if he had said *I love you.*

"Do you want me to stop?" Nate's question, his voice low as he whispered in her ear, made her wriggle beneath him, searching out his eyes.

"No," she whispered back, shaking her head. Sarah hated that he'd taken some of his weight off her, had liked feeling crushed beneath him, his hot breath on her neck, hands skimming her body. "No," she whispered again.

Nate stroked her forehead, his fingers trailing slowly down her face with a delicateness that made her squirm, body shuddering as his thumb dipped into her mouth on its way to her chin.

"Nate." She had no idea why she wanted to keep saying his name, maybe to believe it was real, that this was actually happening.

"You're sure?" he asked.

Damn it, did he have to keep being such a gentleman? Did she have to spell out exactly what she wanted him to do to her? *The thought filled her body with heat.* No way could she talk to him about what she wanted.

Instead, she nodded when his fingers brushed her face, before grazing his lips against hers, his weight against her body again, nestled snug into her. "You're even more beautiful than I remembered," Nate told her, his lips so close to hers as he spoke that she could feel his warm breath against her skin.

Sarah murmured; she wasn't capable of anything else.

"I mean it, Sarah." The look on Nate's face, the tenderness in the way he touched her, like she was the most cherished of possessions that he couldn't bear the thought of hurting, made her heart beat too fast. Made her light-headed, made her crave his touch like she'd die without the attention of his hands on her body. Without his lips cradling hers.

"Nate?" she whispered, pressing him back ever so slightly with one hand.

"Mmm-hmm," he mumbled, pushing her cheek

slightly so that her lips were aligned perfectly beneath his again.

Nate slipped one finger under the strap of her dress, pushing it gently down to expose more skin.

Sarah heard the moan rise from her own throat, arched her back as Nate's lips left hers and started to burn a heat-filled path down her neck, past her collarbone, to her…

"Nate," she managed, choking out his name.

His grin was wicked, a lazy, conceited smile spreading across his face as he stopped, looked up and met her eyes.

"You *do* want me to stop?" he asked.

She giggled, unable to stop herself. "No," she said, her palm cupping his jaw as she stroked his cheek. He was so handsome, so chiseled yet masculine, tough in the most desirable of ways. "I want you to turn the lights out."

He looked like he was about to disagree, to decline her wish, but the devilish grin was back as quick as it had disappeared.

"Follow me," he ordered, pushing against the carpet as he rose to his feet, offering her a hand to do the same.

Sarah hesitated, wasn't sure whether she'd completely ruined the moment or somehow made it better. She took his hand for him to help her up, but Nate swept her off her feet and up into his arms before she could even steady herself.

"What are you doing?" she demanded, wriggling to break free from his grip. But he held her tight, so snug against his chest that she couldn't move an inch.

"I'm taking you to the bedroom," he informed her, the determined look in his eyes making her stomach flip.

She tried wriggling again. "I'm too heavy, your leg…"

His gaze flashed with anger then, his arms tightening even harder around her. "Don't go there," he warned.

Sarah didn't need to be told twice. She scooped

her arms around his neck, hands locking in the air behind him, and offered her mouth to Nate. *And he took it without hesitation.* If he said he could carry her, he could carry her.

"Bedroom?" he asked, voice husky again.

"Yeah." Sarah breathed out the word, her heart racing again, pounding hard.

This time Nate didn't pause to ask if she was sure. He stormed toward his room with a determination that terrified her.

CHAPTER ELEVEN

Sarah lay wrapped in one of Nate's arms, her leg curled over his, head flat to his chest. She'd fallen asleep, too, but something had woken her.

Ow. Nate's comfortable hold on her tightened, his arm squeezing her hard, then releasing again. *At least now she knew why she was awake if he'd done that before.*

Sarah didn't move, not sure what to do. She knew Nate wouldn't hurt her intentionally, but the last time she'd tried to comfort him when he'd been obviously having a dream hadn't exactly worked out that well for her.

His arm tightened again but she stayed still. *She had no idea what to do, whether she should slip away from him and wriggle to the other side of the bed, or stay put and try to comfort him.*

Nate started to shake then and Sarah did move. She wasn't scared of him but…she swallowed and held up a pillow to cuddle, clutched to her naked body. She suddenly felt supervulnerable. His body shuddered violently, one arm thrashed out, but Sarah was still frozen, unsure what to do. When he started to mumble words she couldn't understand, she fumbled and flipped the bedside lamp on, hoping the light would wake him.

But it didn't. All it did was make his distress more obvious. His forehead was glistening with sweat, his body was twisting in the sheets, face pained.

She had to do something.

Sarah edged closer, wished she wasn't naked so she'd feel more confident, but she couldn't take her eyes off Nate. Was powerless to leave him for even a moment, despite the fact she had no idea what to do, how she could help him.

He didn't need to be jolted from sleep, and he

needed to know where he was, who was with him, as soon as he woke.

"It's Sarah," she said, her voice a low whisper, wrapping her arms tight around herself and resisting touching him. Not letting herself wriggle any closer even though her instinct was to hold him, to cocoon him in her arms. "It's Sarah. I'm here, Nate, it's Sarah," she said, braver now, her voice stronger. Nate wasn't thrashing now but his eyes were still shut. The sheets were a tangled mess on his side of the bed.

"It's Sarah, Nate. Sarah," she repeated, still desperate to reach out to him.

Nate woke then, leaped up into a sitting position, his eyes wild, like a stranger sitting before her.

But it was Nate. He wouldn't hurt her, do anything out of character, so long as he knew it was her.

"Nate, it's Sarah, look at me."

The wildness disappeared from Nate's gaze almost immediately. He ran a shaky hand through his hair, looked around, then brought his knees up to his chest, dropping his forehead to rest on them.

Sarah took her cue. He wasn't a danger to her anymore, knew it was her.

"Nate," she whispered, scooting over to him, no longer caring that she was naked. *This was Nate she was with, not some stranger.* Sarah put her arm carefully around his back, her other hand touching his hair.

When he drew back, made eye contact with her, she knew he'd be okay, that she could at least be there for him and that he'd let her.

"You're going to be okay," she told him, her lips to his ear as she held him tight.

Nate's body went stiff, then relaxed, his arms going around her to hug her back.

"Every night," he said, his voice muffled against her hair. "There's not a single night that I go to bed and that doesn't happen."

Sarah swallowed furiously, willing herself not to cry. Nate didn't deserve this sort of pain, not after what he'd been through, what he'd seen… *what he'd done for a friend.* "Are you reliving what happened?" she asked, hoping she wasn't pushing it by asking more.

Nate let go of her and leaned back, his head resting against the wall behind the bed. "I see everything," he told her. "I see Jimmy, I see blood, explosions—you name it, it's in my nightmares."

Sarah lay down, her head nestling into the soft pillow, and held out her hand for Nate to join her. He didn't move to turn off the lamp and neither did she.

Nate lay down beside her, on his side, so they were nose to nose, mouth to mouth. He skimmed the side of her body, running his hand down her arm, over her backside and to the top of her thigh. "I thought that being with you, having you beside me, might help."

She wished it had, too. Now that she'd witnessed what he went through, had seen him transform from peaceful sleeper to a man plagued by night terrors, she could understand why he'd almost strangled her in the state he'd been in. Why he'd mistaken her to be someone from his dreams, and how much it must have hurt him when he'd realized what he'd done.

"I'm not scared of you, Nate, if that's what you're worried about," she said, touching a slow kiss to his lips.

Nate pressed into her, the length of his body fitted to hers. "The other night, when we were drunk and asleep on the sofa, was the first time I've slept through without waking like this."

Wow. "But you haven't woken from a nightmare to this before, have you?" Sarah asked, smiling as she wiggled against him.

Nate chuckled, a deep noise followed by his hand grasping her bottom. "No, Sarah. I haven't."

She pretended to protest, to fight him when he held both her hands down and lay above her, settling enough of his weight over her that she knew she'd never get away even if she wanted to.

"I've never told anyone about this, either," he

whispered, placing a teasing kiss to her neck, then the other side, before finding her mouth. *"Ever."*

She looked into his eyes, could sense the level of trust he was instilling in her. Nate wasn't the kind of man who'd like anyone to know his weaknesses, would never like to burden anyone else with his problems. And she had no intention of divulging anything he told her to anyone, no matter what.

"Your secrets are always safe with me, Nate." *If only she could share her secrets with him.*

Nate woke with a sense of calm that surprised him. Usually, after he'd woken from a night terror, he'd never fall back into a comfortable sleep. It was why his eyes felt like they were hanging from their sockets most days, and probably why his temper was too quick to leap to the surface. Especially where his family were concerned.

He briefly shut his eyes and focused on the softness of the woman lying beside him. *Sarah.*

He'd never imagined he'd be sharing a bed with her again, that he would have her in his arms, that he'd have *loved her* like he had last night.

She sighed in her sleep and moved, snuggling in closer to him. Nate turned so that his arms were around her, studying her face as she stirred. He traced the smoothness of her skin with his eyes, drank in her soft lips, smiled as he slowly reached a hand toward her face and plucked a soft curl that was draped over her cheek.

"Hey," she mumbled, lips parting but her eyes still shut. "I can tell you're looking at me."

Nate put his arm back around Sarah and pulled her closer. Never in a million years, after what he'd been through and the way he'd felt these past few months, had he ever imagined being with Sarah again. Opening up to anyone about his experiences or the secret he held. But she was starting to change the way he thought, the way he behaved. Even if it had been slow progress up until now.

"Sleep well?" he asked.

She grinned and opened her eyes. "Yes. Better than I have in a long while."

Nate touched her cheek with the backs of his fingers. "Divorce keeping you awake at night?"

A look passed across Sarah's face that he couldn't read. But it was one he recognized from that first time he'd seen her, under his tree. Like she was upset, couldn't help from showing it, but wiped the emotion as quick as she could. *But not fast enough for him not to notice.*

"Sarah?"

She shook her head against the pillow, pulling back from him slightly. "It's nothing, Nate."

He wasn't buying it. "If you do need to talk, about Todd, or anything—" he tried hard not to grimace when he said his former friend's name "—I'm here for you just like you were for me."

Sarah wriggled and kissed him, her arm circling his neck. "Thank you," she said.

Nate was curious to know what was wrong, but whatever was keeping her up at night wasn't something she wanted to talk about and he understood exactly what that felt like.

"How about some breakfast?" he suggested, changing the subject so she didn't have to.

Sarah cringed, not exactly the response he'd expected.

"Did I say something wrong?" he asked, rising and pulling on the jeans that he'd shed way too fast the night before. They were crumpled in a heap on the floor.

"Oh, my God." Sarah's hand flew to her mouth, sitting up and drawing the sheets to cover herself.

Nate's eyebrow shot up in question. "What?"

"You never struck me as the commando type." She giggled.

He planted his hands on the bed and leaned toward her, kissing her before grabbing the sheet between his teeth and pulling it away from her.

"Nate!"

He laughed and jumped back. "I'll have you know it's only a morning kind of thing. I didn't know how fast you'd want to be ripping off my pants again, so I thought I'd make it easy for you."

Sarah rolled her eyes, but he didn't miss the pink blush as it frosted her cheeks. He didn't remember her blushing so much when they'd been together even though she'd been a whole lot younger then, but she seemed to do it all the time now.

"I'll have you know that it was you who initi-ated—" she paused and held the sheet up again to cover her breasts "—*this.*"

Nate stood and walked to the door, before turning back. "What was it you were going to tell me before?"

She sighed and Nate wished he'd just forgot-ten about it and not asked.

"I had a phone call from Todd before I ar-rived here last night. He confirmed our meet-ing today."

Nate nodded, probably for longer than he needed to. "You still want me to be there?"

Sarah smiled, meekly this time. "Yeah, but only if it's not a problem. I mean, if you have something else on, or you need to be somewhere..."

Nate gave her a quick salute, followed by what he hoped was a convincing smile. "I'll be there."

They stared at each other for a moment before Nate remembered where he'd been heading. "I hope you like omelets," he called out as he walked away from her. "'Cause it's all I know how to make!"

Nate reached the kitchen and leaned against the wall, needing a minute to think about what he'd just agreed to. He did want to help Sarah, but the reality of seeing Todd again wasn't exactly appealing, even though he'd told her yesterday that he'd do it for her.

He still had so many issues to deal with, was struggling with his own problems, but Sarah had been there for him and he'd promised the same of her.

Nate opened a drawer to find the utensils he

needed, but his fingers first connected with a folded piece of paper. *Jimmy's wife. What he needed to do today was muster the courage to phone her.*

He pushed it to the side, like he'd been doing for months, and set about making breakfast. Maybe he should tell Sarah, or maybe he should just quit stalling and do something about it.

CHAPTER TWELVE

SARAH was beside-herself nervous. Nate was sitting on her sofa and surfing the channels on her television, and she was starting to pace. Was he seriously okay with this kind of normality? And what had the verdict been on whether they were still pretending or not? Because what had happened between them had her seriously confused, and if they were starting something here, then she needed to get something off her chest.

Argh. Being with Nate, dealing with Todd, it was all too much.

"Nate," she said, straightening her shoulders and moving to stand in front of him. He laughed and leaned around her to use the remote, switching the television off.

"Come here," he said, trying to loop his fingers into her jeans and tug her down.

"Nate!" she scolded, standing her ground. "I'm trying to be serious here."

"So am I."

She swatted at his hand, almost wishing things didn't feel so good between them. She should have just told him to start with, admitted why Todd's having a baby had upset her so much when she'd first found out.

Moose couldn't resist any longer and leaped up, nosing at her like he was making sure she was okay. He'd been watching Nate with a wary expression ever since he'd arrived, but after spending the night before being babysat by her mom, he seemed pretty pleased to be home.

"Shoot," he said, pulling her down slowly so she could sit on the arm of the chair. "And tell that dog that he's going to have to get used to me."

She wished that was all she had on her mind, worrying about her overprotective dog not liking

Nate when animals usually loved him, but she needed to get this off her chest. It was time she was honest with Nate, opened up to him about what had happened to *her* these past few years, the pain she'd been through. Telling him now before things went any further between them, before she risked being hurt again, was the only way forward. Especially after he'd been so brave talking to her.

"Sarah?" he asked, his playful expression turning into a frown as he watched her.

"Nate, there's something I—"

"Well, isn't this cozy."

Sarah leaped up and nearly tripped over her rug at the sound of Todd's voice. "Have you heard of knocking?" she demanded, furious that he'd just walked in like that when it wasn't his home to do so anymore.

Todd looked at her, then back at Nate, eyes wide with what she could only guess was disbelief. Sarah dropped her hand to her dog's head when she heard his low growl, which turned into a muttered whine at her touch.

"From memory I'm pretty sure the house is still half-mine, so I didn't know I had to knock," Todd said, watching Nate closely. "But then I wasn't exactly expecting to find you shacked up with someone so soon."

Sarah tried to stay calm, didn't want to engage in a fight with Todd and especially not in front of Nate, but she was so angry her hands had started to shake. "Todd, let's not argue, and please don't accuse me of anything when you've hardly been the world's best role model, okay? I saw you with your fiancée in town and I guessed she'd be with you today."

If she was angry, Todd looked wild. "All these years I knew you were pining over *him*, but I tried to tell myself it was stupid. That you weren't still in love with a guy who'd decided he had better things to do than come back to you."

"I think that's enough, Todd." Nate's deep, commanding voice sent a shiver through her.

"Don't you tell me what to do in my house to *my wife*." Todd was red-faced and beyond angry now, the testosterone and tension in the room overwhelming.

Tears fell down Sarah's cheeks and she couldn't stop them, but Nate's body beside hers when he rose, his hand on her hip, made her stand strong. Todd was the one at fault here, not her, and she wasn't going to be made out to be the bad guy. She had been faithful to him and done everything she could during their marriage, to make it work, and while she'd thought of Nate often she'd never treated Todd like she didn't love him.

"Todd, I signed the divorce papers and sent them back yesterday. I think you'll find that I'm no longer your wife." Her voice was cooler, calmer, than she'd expected. "You've moved on, and now so have I."

Todd stood there, glaring at her and Nate like he wanted to set them on fire with his gaze alone. Why was he even angry when he'd so clearly moved on?

"Was this going on during our marriage?" Todd demanded, directing the question at her and pointing at Nate.

Sarah shook her head. "No." From the corner of her eye she could see the determined look in Nate's eyes, the hard line of his jaw as he kept his mouth clamped shut, like he was desperate to interfere and put Todd in his place, but trying so hard to let her deal with the situation on her own. "You were the unfaithful one, Todd, not me. I never did anything other than try to make things work between us."

Todd started to walk backward to the door, like he'd had enough, his expression pure hatred, but not yet ready to turn away. "Have you told him the truth yet, Sarah?"

Her lip quivered but she took a step toward him, praying that he'd stop, that he wouldn't tell Nate. But he only sensed her discomfort and laughed, like he couldn't wait to make a fool of her, to make sure she didn't find happiness with anyone else. He'd been so cruel toward her at the end when she'd been trying so hard to make things work, to deal with what she was going through, coming to terms with how the news from her doctor would change her life forever.

"Todd, please," she begged, shaking her head and pleading with him as she looked him in the eye.

"Ah, I see. Lover boy doesn't know that the happy little family you were always talking about before he left can't happen. That you'll never be able to have his kids. I wonder if he'll still want you now, sweetheart?"

His cruelty made her feel like she'd just been cut in half. She'd come to dislike him at the end of the marriage, been furious for what he'd done, but she'd never known he could be so full of hatred, that he could want to hurt her that bad for something she'd had no control over.

"Just go, Todd. Get out of my house," she said, her voice so quiet that she wondered if he'd even heard her. "The next time you want to discuss our settlement you can do it through my lawyer. I'm done playing nice."

He walked out and left her standing there, wishing she'd never asked Nate to be witness to their meeting. She should have known how badly Todd would react to him, even if he did have a new partner and baby on the way. Nate's had always been a name that wasn't mentioned in their house, for the very reason that they had a history together that everyone in the district knew about, especially Todd. She'd been stupid asking Nate to come, even if it had seemed like the right thing to do at the time.

"Sarah?"

Nate's hand on her back told her it wasn't all just a bad nightmare, either. *It was real.*

"Just go, Nate. Please." She couldn't face him, not after being humiliated like that.

Nate walked around her when she refused to turn so she couldn't ignore him. "Sarah?" He tried to tilt her chin but she looked away.

"I'm sorry you had to witness that, but Todd's

right," she told him, in a voice far braver than she felt inside. "I can't have children, Nate, so whatever happened between us last night doesn't mean we can just pick up and go back to what we used to have. I'll never carry a child, not with you, not with *anyone*."

She couldn't read Nate's expression and she didn't want to. Maybe he'd just wanted to have some fun, maybe he wasn't thinking the same things that she'd been hoping, wishing they could step back in time. But if she knew Nate like she thought she did, he wouldn't have just slept with her if it didn't mean something, not with the history they shared. And he'd be furious that she hadn't opened up to him, especially when she'd been so demanding of him facing up to his issues.

"You should have told me," he said.

Sarah met his gaze, defiant. "Why? You had enough of your own problems to deal with without me off-loading mine. I can't ever get pregnant, Nate. Not now, not ever." She shouldn't have been angry with him, but she was. Or maybe she was just angry with herself. "But I'm at peace with that now."

He shook his head, his expression sad. "I'm sure there are plenty of specialists, or doctors you could talk to. There must be—"

"Stop, Nate, just stop," she ordered, battling tears again. "Don't you think I've done everything I can? That I've investigated every possible way for me to have a baby? I can't and there's nothing anyone can do for me, okay?"

He nodded. "I'm sorry."

"Well, I don't want your pity and I don't want you to pretend like it doesn't matter, so I think you should just go."

He shuffled toward her, arms open. "Sarah, I know you're hurt but—"

"But what, Nate? You want a family, and so do I, but we can't ever have one together. Not like we always talked about, anyway. I've been with a man who said it was okay, and now look at him? Shacked up with another woman already and about to become a dad." She took a big breath and let it out on a slow exhale. "You have no idea how he treated me when he found out, after we'd exhausted every option and I *still* couldn't get pregnant. So I'd rather never put myself through that again."

Now it was Nate who looked angry. "I'd never treat you the way Todd just did, *never*. You know that, Sarah, and if you don't, then you don't know me at all."

"But?" she asked.

"What do you mean, *but?*"

Sarah touched his cheek before she walked away from him. "But you still want to be a dad, Nate. You might say *no* now, but I've seen the way you are with Brady. *I know you,* and you're going to make someone a great husband and be a great father one day. Of your own biological children."

He stared at her, his expression like carved stone.

"Maybe I was right, then. Maybe you don't

know me at all." Nate gave her a look she'd never seen before—a sad, haunted expression that sent an icy blast through her body. Chilled her to the bone and made her wish she'd just kept her mouth shut.

And then he did exactly as she'd asked and walked out her door.

Sarah dropped to her knees and curled up beside her dog, the tears falling freely now. She could deal with her marriage being over, but she didn't know if she'd ever cope with losing Nate. *Not again.*

CHAPTER THIRTEEN

NATE was in a foul mood, but he didn't want to take his anger out on anyone or anything. Which was why he was sitting on the sofa on an otherwise perfect afternoon, instead of riding or helping out on the ranch. He should have gone out and found Holt, but given his recent track record, he didn't want to say something to his brother that he could regret later.

He was fuming about Sarah and trying not to think about her simultaneously, and it wasn't working. He couldn't give a crap about her not being able to have children, except for the fact that he hated how deeply she must have hurt when she'd found out. What he was furious about was her not telling him, not opening up to him. That he'd had to find out from Todd.

Nate looked up, stared at the kitchen, before rising. If he was going to sit around inside, he needed to do something productive, and he knew exactly what that something was. If Sarah had taught him one thing, it was that he needed to be honest, to deal with his emotions and not push people away. Well, there was one person he should be offering a helping hand to, and she deserved at least a phone call from him.

Nate strode across the room and pulled out the piece of paper. He reached for the phone and dialed the number, wishing he could stop his hand from shaking.

She answered almost immediately.

Nate swallowed and tried to push the memories away, tried to stop thinking about Jimmy and how he'd looked when he'd died. What it was like seeing his best friend lying with blood seeping from him.

No. He was stronger than that. He had to be.

"Lucy, it's Nate. I've been meaning to call you for months now."

The kind, gentle voice at the other end settled his nerves.

He wasn't going to tell her the truth about how Jimmy's life had ended, but he was going to tell her about how brave her husband had been leading up to that day, and why he'd been such a good friend when Nate had needed him most.

That he'd done his best to save Jimmy, to be there for him, and that Jimmy had had his back on every mission they'd been on. Not the last one, but in Nate's books that didn't count. Jimmy had been his best friend, and his best friend's widow deserved to know just how damn special her husband had been.

Sarah walked slowly with her dog, as far away from the dwelling as possible. She didn't even want to make eye contact with the guesthouse Nate was living in, and she sure as heck wasn't going to look over at his tree. The one they'd sat under together so many times, and the place where she'd found him such a short time ago.

She missed him like hell already and she didn't want to think about him.

"Come on, Moose," she called.

Sarah came to the gate closest to where her horse was grazing and she let her dog through before doing the same. Then froze on the spot. From where she was standing she could see Johnny and Brady, and *there was Nate.* Playing with his nephew, touching his hand to his head, before mounting one of Johnny's horses.

Where was he going?

Sarah stayed still, hoping Nate wouldn't turn around and see her standing there, and he didn't. As soon as he was out of eyesight she made her way over to Maddie and took hold of her halter, before leading her toward the far gate so she could get her gear and saddle up.

She bit her lip and kept walking, waving out to Johnny as he turned around. Just because things were through before they'd started with Nate didn't mean she was going to stop riding. She loved the Calhoun family and Holt hadn't seemed to mind her horse spending some time here over the summer, so that wasn't going to change.

She had to forget Nate all over again, no matter how much it hurt. Her future wasn't going to be what she'd hoped it would be, but she was going to do her best to move on. She owed it to herself, and she owed it to Nate to let him go.

Nate was starting to regret not bringing more clothing. Johnny had told him to watch the weather, and now after an hour of riding he wished he'd heeded his warnings. There was a storm brewing—he could feel it in his bones—and that meant he needed to get back fast. He might have been away from Texas for a few years, but he'd never forgotten the thunderstorms that could blast a tree in two, even in the middle of summer.

He'd taken the stirrups off completely today instead of crossing them over the pommel of his saddle or letting them swing free, and it had been the right decision. He was able to nudge the horse into a canter without worrying about them, and it made it easier on his leg. He could grip with his knees and not put any pressure on his lower leg, and so long as he could keep his balance he'd make it home, fast, before the worst of the storm hit.

As they settled into a steady rhythm the first raindrops fell, heavy plops that soaked straight through his shirt. Nate urged his horse on, forgetting everything other than the stretch and pull of the animal beneath him.

"Easy," he called, one hand touching the horse's neck as a low rumble of thunder sounded out.

She calmed for a moment and then pulled on his hands, fighting for her head. Then Nate saw what she was becoming so excited about. There was another horse in the distance, *a rider in trouble.* Nate didn't ask his horse to go any faster, with no stirrups they were already cantering too fast, so he did his best to keep her steady and calm.

And then he recognized the horse and rider. *It was Sarah, and she was only just managing to stay in the saddle.* Shit. This was not good weather to take a freshly broken horse out in. What the hell did she think she was doing?

"Steady, girl," he told his mount, "nice and steady." He asked his horse to slow as they approached, sitting deeper in the saddle and being firmer with his hands. "Whoa."

"Nate!" Sarah's usually calm voice was ear-piercingly high.

"Stay calm," he ordered, asking his horse to walk slowly toward Sarah and her nervous mount. "Get those shoulders back and tell her who's boss." He might be a fan of natural horsemanship, but the horse still had to know who was in charge, and right now Sarah wasn't doing a very good job of making that clear. They were flight animals; if she wasn't assertive, the situation was going to get dangerous.

He neared the skittish horse and made a grab for the reins, trying to keep his balance. Damn it!

If his leg wasn't buggered he would have jumped off and taken hold of the young mare and settled her, instead of struggling to even keep control of his own horse. *But then if he wasn't injured, maybe he would never have come home.*

"Hey, girl," he said, pulling back hard to keep Sarah's horse steady. "We're okay."

Another rumble of thunder followed by a crack of lightning made the horse's eyes roll and Nate was finding it harder to stay in the saddle, especially with his own horse becoming jumpy.

"Sarah, you okay?"

He glanced at her quickly, saw the terror in her face, how white her cheeks were.

"Don't let go, Nate."

"Come on," he said firmly. "We need to either get back right now or unsaddle the horses and let them go. It's your call." He hoped she agreed on the first option, but he'd do whatever she was most comfortable with. If she was that frozen with fear, riding back might not even be an option. "Sarah?"

"Let's go," she agreed.

Nate took control, not wanting to take any risks, not where Sarah was concerned. "Let's start at the walk. If we can keep them calm enough, we'll trot back."

Sarah nodded and he saw the determined look in her eyes that had been missing before. The glint that he usually associated with her attitude to everything she did, her confidence returning.

Sarah's horse jig-jogged, nervous as hell, but she stuck to his mount like glue, not wanting to break away on her own. "We're going to be fine," he called to her, raising his voice over the now-insistent drops of rain and rumblings of the fast-approaching storm. "She's not going to break away from my horse and I think we need to speed things up." At this rate, Nate knew they didn't have a chance at making it back to the house or stables. But there was a barn they could get to, where they'd all be safe, *so long as lightning didn't strike too close.*

"You okay trotting?" she asked.

Nate gritted his teeth together as they broke into a fast trot. Given the fact he had no stirrups, bouncing along wasn't exactly his favorite gait. "How about we canter?"

He could see her confidence had returned, at least temporarily. "I'll give it a go."

The horses were jumpy but they rode side by side, the rain starting to pelt down and soak through his shirt. Nate saw the barn he'd had in mind, somewhere they usually stored hay at the end of each season if they had need to, and one he hoped was empty. He pointed to Sarah, his eyes blurry from rain as he gestured where they were heading. They both slowed to a trot, then a walk, pulling up outside it. They never would have made it back to the stables or close to the house.

"Let's dismount and lead them in. There's a few old wooden gates in there and a center divide, so if you're okay holding them I'll erect a makeshift stall for the pair of them," he called out to Sarah, stretching his legs and rotating his ankle before swinging his leg over his horse and landing with a thud on the wet earth below.

Son of a... Nate swallowed the curses ready to burst from his mouth. Damn it if his leg didn't hurt like hell, but he had a task to do and no time to fool around. Sarah was already on the ground, watching him, her eyes asking questions even though she didn't actually say a thing.

"Here," he said, passing her the reins. "I'll make it quick." Nate wanted to get out of the rain but he also wanted to get Sarah out of harm's way, and he wasn't convinced she'd be able to keep hold of both horses, who were leaping around like a pair of idiots, if the storm came so much as an inch closer.

Nate limped into the open barn, grabbing an old ball of string and dragging two of the old gates leaning against one of the walls. He tied them together and hauled a few of last season's bales of hay over, too. "Bring them in," he called out.

Sarah started toward him but lightning cracked

close by, making her horse rear up in fright. Nate made it to her just in time, grabbing her horse. "Whoa, girl, let's get inside." His voice was firm and so was his hold as he led her in. Sarah brought his horse in and he passed her the reins again, before hauling the hay bales into the gap and building them up.

"Shall we take their bridles off?" Sarah asked, her voice shaky.

Nate gave her what he hoped was a confident smile. "Nope. Let's put the reins back over their heads and knot them. That way if they get away they won't break their necks tripping over them, and we can still get hold of them quick if we need to."

Sarah climbed over the gates with a hand from Nate once they'd settled the horses as much as they could. He'd passed some decent-looking hay over, which was keeping them happy for now, even if they were still understandably frightened.

She went to let go of Nate's hand, then grabbed it again, her legs wobbly. She could have been badly injured out there, could have had a bad fall and been left out in the storm for hours or even longer before anyone found her. *She'd been trying to avoid Nate and somehow he'd ended up saving her.*

"I should never have ridden out in that weather. Johnny warned me, but all I could think about was needing to get up in the saddle and clear my head," she admitted to Nate. "I'm not usually one to take risks, but…" She didn't even know what to say. Thank goodness she'd left Moose behind to play with Brady; the last thing she'd have needed was him to worry about, as well.

He put an arm around her, but she could tell from the awkward angle he was on that something was wrong. "You're okay now, so don't even think about it. Maybe we should both listen to Johnny more often, though—sounds like he has better brains than the pair of us combined."

"Nate?"

He looked at her. They'd both stopped walking.

"Your leg's bugging you, isn't it?" she asked.

Nate steered her toward some hay bales and sat down, his leg stretched out in front of him. "Bugging me would be an understatement," he admitted. "Hurting me like someone's stabbing me over and over in the calf might be a better description."

Her shocked expression as she sat down beside him made him laugh.

"Okay, maybe I shouldn't have been quite so honest. I'm fine, Sarah, please don't worry about me."

She shook her head, slowly, before tucking her knees up and wrapping her arms around her legs. Now that they were sitting, the adrenaline rush of riding and securing the horses over, she'd realized how cold she was. Her shirt and jeans were sodden, completely soaked through, and it was taking an effort to stop her teeth from chattering. The last thing she needed was to be miserable and get sick, too.

"Great summer weather, huh?" Nate asked.

She nodded. "Yeah."

They sat there, not saying anything, the only noise the pounding tap on the roof as the rain fell furiously, the storm surrounding them. Sarah stared into the torrential rain, watched the jagged lightning in the sky as it lit everything around it.

"Come here." The softness of Nate's voice made her look up. "I'd come to you but…" He pointed at his leg. "It might be easier for you to come to me."

Sarah wanted to resist, didn't want to be close to Nate, to remind herself of what she was missing out on. *But she couldn't.*

Sarah stood and crossed the distance between them, sitting down beside him. Nate's arm automatically went around her, pulling her tight against his body. Letting her steal some of his warmth, even though he was as wet as she was.

"You're freezing," he said, sitting up more and putting his other arm around her to try to warm her up.

Sarah wasn't going to deny how cold she was, especially with the heat coming off Nate. She had no idea how he could still be so warm given the storm they'd both been stuck out in.

"Why aren't you freezing, too?"

He chuckled. "I am, but I'm kind of used to extreme temperatures. I've been trained for years to cope with this sort of situation, and I've seen a lot worse. Sometimes heat is worse than the cold."

"Nate?" she asked, burying her face against his shoulder, not strong enough to pull herself away from him. *She should have stayed on the other side of the barn, but there wasn't a chance she was going back there now.*

"Yeah?" His mouth was touching the top of her head, her hair.

"I'm sorry about your friend, and about your leg, too. I wish things were different for you." She didn't know why, but telling him how she felt, what she'd been wanting to say to him and not known how to, seemed to take a weight off her shoulders.

Nate grunted, half chuckle, half throat-clear. "Me, too." He hugged her closer and she held on tight. "And I'm sorry about the whole baby thing, as well." Nate's voice was low and husky, like he hadn't known what to say or whether to mention it.

"Me, too," she said, listening to the steady beat of his heart through his wet shirt, enjoying the constant rhythm against her ear. "Me, too." She'd had a while to come to terms with it now, but the reality that she'd never be able to have a baby with a man she loved one day still hurt sometimes.

Nate let go of her with one arm and started to stroke her hair. She shut her eyes and leaned into him, craving him more than she'd ever like to admit, even to herself.

"Sarah, just because you can't have children doesn't mean you can't be a mom," he said. She squeezed her eyes shut even tighter. "You could easily adopt one day. Don't give up on your dreams just because the journey's too hard— there are plenty of kids out there in the world in need of a great mom. If it's what you want, I know you can make it happen."

What did she say to that? Of course she knew her options, but hearing it from someone else, *from Nate,* was kind of reassuring. That it wasn't just some line she'd been feeding herself to make herself feel better. "Thanks, Nate."

He pushed back from her. "Let me finish."

A loud bang of thunder made her jump back into his arms, pressed tight to his side. The horses were starting to skitter, too, kicking against the side of the barn.

"Settle down, girls. We're all okay," Nate called out to them, rising slightly to look in at them. "No need to be scared."

Sarah fiddled with the hem of her wet shirt, hating that they were stuck here, soaking, and having a conversation she'd rather not be engaging in. She could feel him watching her, then his hands covered hers to stop her nervous fiddling.

"Just because one man couldn't deal with your infertility doesn't mean you're not going to meet someone else. Someone different," he told her. "You have options, and *you* deserve someone who can understand that."

She looked up, met his gaze and stared into his bright blue eyes. "Maybe you're right, but right now I think I might be better on my own. Given my current track record."

The left side of his mouth kicked up into a curve. "Or maybe you're just not giving the right guy a chance."

Sarah's heart started to beat too fast. Her mouth became way too dry for her liking. She needed to deal with this right now, tell him how wrong he was before the conversation went any further. Before he said something, or did something, that would stop her from telling him how she felt.

"Nate, I've seen you with Brady. I know how great you'd be as a dad, and I don't want us to…"

She shrugged, pulling her hands back from his and forming a knot with them instead. "I can't deal with losing you again and I know we can't work."

He glowered at her. "And you think that's a decision you can make on your own? Without asking me how I feel?"

Sarah bit down hard on her lip, wishing she could walk away. A quick glance out at the storm told her otherwise. The rain was so thick and hitting the ground hard, so there was no chance of escape. Especially if she didn't want to risk becoming lost or zapped by a lightning bolt, not to mention hypothermic if her body temperature dropped any lower.

"Let's not make this harder than it has to be. What we used to have was great, seeing you again has been amazing, but we don't have a real future together."

He touched her cheek, shuffling closer, forcing her to stare back at him. "Don't tell me that," he said. "I don't care if you can't have kids, I don't care what's happened in the past. What I care about right now is *you*." He smiled. "*You and only you,* Sarah. When I told you that I loved you, I meant it."

"Nate, if you left me again…" Sarah's voice quavered. *She wasn't ready for this, wasn't prepared to have this sort of discussion.*

"I'm not going to. At least not like that."

She had no idea what he meant, but…

Nate's mouth met hers so fast she didn't have time to think, to push him away. His lips were soft against hers, warm, taking all the cold from her body and replacing it with heat. He kissed her hard, like he didn't ever want to stop, and she didn't ever want to let him.

When Nate pulled away, his lips hovering over hers, she didn't move a muscle.

"When you reminded me the other day about my dreams, what I used to want, you were right," he said, touching his nose to hers before sitting back. "I want to do something on the land, think about the tourist stuff we used to brainstorm about. I don't know, horse trails or luxury camp-ing or *something* that makes money and lets me stay around here and be useful."

Sarah placed her hands on her lap now, trying to stay calm. Her stomach was still full of flip-flops, but she wasn't as nervous as she had been. She wanted to hear what he had to say, even if it scared her. She owed it to herself to listen.

"What I need is some time to figure out what I want, Sarah. What I want to do with my life."

She wasn't sure what he was trying to tell her, if he was asking her something. "You need to do whatever feels right, Nate."

He grinned at her. "What feels right is us, *you,*" he told her. "But as much as I want this to work, I need to sort myself out first. Otherwise I have nothing to offer you. I need a month, Sarah. A month of figuring things out and spending time on my own, so we both know where we stand and what our future could be."

Her hands had started to shake. *Had she heard*

him right? "I don't understand. Do you still want to be with me?"

Nate opened his arms and pulled her into his chest. "More than ever. If you can forgive me for leaving you all those years ago, I promise I'll spend the rest of my life making it up to you."

Sarah looked up at him, her arms wrapped around herself and her back twisted so she could stare up at his face. "I forgive you, Nate. Of course I forgive you." *How could she not?* Truth be told, she'd forgiven him a long time ago, because the years she'd spent with him had been the best of her life.

He laughed and dropped a kiss to her head. "And no more baby talk, okay? I need you to know that I don't give a damn about you not being able to have kids. Right?"

She shut her eyes, hoping he wouldn't regret what he was saying. She knew how much he loved children; watching him with Brady was reason enough to see that he would be a great dad. "But if you do…"

He tilted her chin back up with his thumb. "I won't. What I want is you. And if it becomes something we both want, then we'll do something about it. Okay? We can find a kid who really needs us, who's already out there in the world." He sighed. "I saw plenty of children when I was away, kids in desperate need of someone to love them, so I'd love to help even one child, one day. To do something out of love."

She shook her head. He'd managed to amaze her again. "I can't even imagine what you've seen, Nate, what you've been through."

He dropped another kiss to her head, and she didn't pry. He'd keep opening up to her, when he was ready; she just had to be patient.

Sarah looked outside, suddenly realizing that there was no longer a constant drumbeat of rain in the background. The storm had passed as fast as it had arrived. Where else but Texas would a summer storm like *that* hit?

"Nate, it's over," she told him, gesturing with her head.

He grunted like he wasn't that happy about it, so she kept hold of him, tucked against him. She might have wanted to run before, but now that all the hard stuff was behind them, the discussion she'd been so scared of having now out in the open, staying with Nate in the barn wasn't sounding like such a bad idea.

"When you said you wanted a month…"

"I want to leave here and travel around a bit, see what my competition is in the tourism industry and take some time to get my head in the right place," he told her.

So where did that leave them? What did he actually want?

"But," he continued, as if he could sense her question, "it doesn't change the way I feel about you. I need you to know that. Sorting my head out is about dealing with what happened to me back in Black Ops. I want to visit Jimmy's widow and go to his grave, spend time on some other ranches and see what they do. Me going away is not for thinking about whether or not I want to come home to you, Sarah. Because right now that's the only thing I *do* have clear in my mind." Sarah smiled at him when he looked at her. "When I said I wasn't going to leave you again, I meant it."

Sarah shivered in her still-wet shirt. "But if you do…"

"I won't," he insisted. "What I want is for you to deal with your divorce, make sure this is what *you* want. So that we can both start over."

The horses were starting to stomp again, their cue that it was time to get a move on.

"And you're sure about this?" Sarah asked, her cheeks flushing as Nate rose and then pulled her to her feet, so she landed smack-bang against him. *It sounded too good to be true, like she was imagining the words he was saying to her so openly.*

"What I'm sure about is that I love you, Sarah. I love you now and I always have."

Sarah giggled like the first time he'd told her,

under the tree that they'd spent so many hours making out beneath. "I love you, too, Nate."

"Then promise me that we're going to make a real go of this. Of us," he asked, arms slung around her waist to keep them locked together.

"I promise," she told him, tilting her head back for another kiss. "I promise."

And she did. This was Nate, *the love-of-her-life Nate.*

And he'd finally come home for good.

CHAPTER FOURTEEN

SARAH stood on the steps of her porch, watching as Nate loaded his two bags into the trunk of his car. Her hands were starting to shake so she linked them behind her back. This was tough. The last time she'd said goodbye to Nate, he'd never come home to her. And now she had to take a huge leap of faith and believe that this time was going to be different.

"I think that's all," he said, joining her on the porch.

Sarah nodded, starting to panic. "And you definitely have to go, right?"

Nate chuckled and pulled her hands away from her back, slinging them behind him instead. They stood pelvis to pelvis, Nate's head dipping down slightly so he could gaze straight into her eyes.

"I love you, Sarah. You do know that, right?" Nate's voice was low, like he was struggling with leaving her as much as she was struggling with being left.

"I know," she mumbled. *And she did know; he'd made it more than clear. But it didn't help how she was feeling right now.*

"I promise I'll be back by the end of the month. You don't have to worry about me coming home, because there's no part of me that doesn't want to come back to you." He paused, dropping a soft, slow kiss to her lips. "And that's a promise."

She could have held on to him all day, kept her body pressed to his and snuggled close for hours, but she knew she had to let him go. "I'll be fine, it's just…"

"You're worrying it'll be like last time?" he finished for her.

Sarah nodded. "I know it won't be, but part of me keeps thinking that maybe this is the last time I'll see you."

Nate sighed, kissed her again, before stepping

back. Just enough so that his arms were free. He took her hands into his and raised them up, slowly kissing each of her knuckles before meeting her stare again.

"You're the best thing that's ever happened to me, Sarah. I need you to know that," he said. "And when I come back, there's something I'd like very much to place on this finger." Nate plucked at one of the fingers on her left hand with his teeth, before grinning up at her.

"Don't forget about the festival, either?" she joked, blushing furiously after his ring comment and ignoring it simultaneously. "You have to come back to meet your new siblings and help me organize all the finishing touches. Not to mention the dedication to your dad."

Nate groaned. "Are you sure we can't skip the festival and go away somewhere instead? I'm not that sure about meeting all these new people."

Sarah swatted at him, aiming to punch him in the arm, but he grabbed her hand before she'd managed to connect. "I'll have you know that your new sister, Ellie, is a good friend of mine now. What's she going to think when I tell her you've skipped town already without meeting her?"

He didn't seem to care what she said. "Come here," he ordered, keeping hold of her hand.

"I do care, you know that. But what I care about most is you." Nate put his arms around her and held her tight, his face buried in her hair. "I'll be home before you know it, and I'll phone you as soon as I get to Jimmy's house."

Sarah gave him one last squeeze, shut her eyes and tried to lock the way he felt in her arms into her memory. "I love you, Nate."

"Baby, I love you, too."

He walked down the porch steps and stopped at the bottom, turning around to blow her one final kiss. "I'll see you soon."

Sarah nodded and held on to the railing. A wet nose nudged her hand and she looked down to see Moose now sitting beside her. She couldn't help but laugh at him, staring down at Nate like he was pleased to be rid of him, like he was the man of the house and he didn't like being challenged.

"You better train that dog to like me before I get back!" Nate called out to her, waving through the open window.

Sarah was laughing so hard she couldn't even manage to answer him.

Who would have thought she'd ever be sharing a laugh with Nate Calhoun again, let alone waving him goodbye and waiting for him to return?

EPILOGUE

SARAH walked out to check the mailbox. The sun was bright so she held up her hand as she peered inside, not expecting to find anything other than a bill inside. She was wrong. She pulled out the card, smiling to herself at the rodeo scene depicted on the front.

Nate. She flipped the card and looked at the familiar writing on the back. Messier than it had been when they'd written to each other while he was away serving, but she'd still recognize it anywhere.

Her heart started to race, then fell back to a more steady rhythm. *So much for being home by the end of the month.* She'd hoped to only have a few more nights without him, but from what he was telling her on the card, she doubted she'd see him for a while yet.

"Come on, Moose," she called to her dog, turning to walk back inside.

"And here I was thinking you'd be pleased to see me."

Sarah stopped. Stood dead still, knowing it couldn't be him. That the deep, teasing voice she'd just heard had to be her imagination, because Nate must still be hours away from Larkville. If not farther.

She spun slowly on the spot.

Oh, my God. "Nate!" She laughed and walked toward him, not letting herself run at him and throw herself into his arms like she wanted to. "But I just got your…" She held up the postcard in one hand as she stepped into his open arms to explain her confusion.

"I just put it in your mailbox. I wanted to see how disappointed you'd look if I told you I wasn't coming home yet. You know, just to make sure you were still into me."

Sarah didn't hold back when he bent to kiss her, looped her arms around his neck and let her lips dance across his, even though she should have told him off for his prank. "You are *so* mean," she murmured, pulling back so she could look up at him. See that it was really him.

"Distance can make a guy worry," he confessed, slipping his fingers into the loops of her jeans.

"Well, you didn't have to worry about me," she said with a sigh, standing on tiptoe and kissing him again. "Not at all."

Now it was Nate clearing his throat and moving away from her. He looked...*nervous.* Sarah watched him closely, wondering what was wrong. Oh, no, had he had a change of heart? Was that what this was about?

"Sarah, I'd hoped to speak to your mom first but now that I've seen you I don't think I can wait." Nate was smiling but his eyes were darting around, like he was nervous, and Nate was *never* nervous.

"Is everything okay? Do I need to sit down?" What was he going to tell her?

Nate's shoulders rose up, then came down. "No."

Sarah closed the distance between them. "Whatever it is, Nate, you can tell me."

He laughed and pulled something from his pocket. He held his little finger out to her, a big smile on his face.

There, perched on the smaller half of his finger, was a ring. A diamond surrounded by a cluster of smaller diamonds that threaded all the way around the band.

"Wow." Sarah couldn't take her eyes from it, not even to look at Nate. It was amazing.

"I don't want to push you if you're not ready, but I love you, Sarah. Always have and always will." Nate's voice was tender, his words making tears flood her vision almost immediately. "This is me telling you," he said, taking her hand and placing the ring in her open palm, before closing her fingers around it, "that I will never leave you ever again. That I love you for *you*."

Sarah stared up into Nate's eyes, shaking her

head slowly from side to side as his words sunk in. She opened her palm and looked at the ring sitting there, before slipping it onto her finger.

Nate's hand nudged her chin up, forcing her to confront his gaze. "Marry me, Sarah? You don't have to say yes now, you don't even have to wear the ring yet if you don't want to, but I want to make my intentions clear." His mouth met hers, lips so tender and soft that she found herself clutching on to his shirt, trying to pull him closer. "I want you to be my wife. *For now and forever.*"

Tears did fall then. She couldn't help it. They trickled freely down her cheeks and Sarah was powerless to do anything about them.

"Yes, Nate. Of course my answer is yes."

His eyes widened. "It is?"

"Yes, I want to marry you, Nate," she said with a laugh, finding it hard to believe that he was even standing in front of her, let alone proposing. "Yes, yes, yes!"

Nate grabbed her around the waist and swung her around, his smile as wide as hers felt.

There was something different about him, something more open and happy about Nate than before he'd left, and she liked it. As if the more grown-up Nate that she'd fallen in love with since he'd returned had merged with the old Nate, the happy young man she'd loved since she was a teenager.

"I think we should take this inside," he whispered in her ear. "I'd hate to upset your neighbors."

Sarah tilted her head back and giggled as he kissed her neck. "There's one problem," she told him.

A low growl echoed out behind them, as if Moose had read her mind.

"If you'd warned me you were coming home, I'd have spent more time training someone to like you."

Nate held her up in his arms, spinning her

around so she faced her dog. "Are you sure we can't find him a new home?"

Sarah gave him a pretend slap across the face, suppressing a squeal when he grabbed her hand and stole a kiss from her.

"Nate, he's my baby," she complained, smiling down at her dog. "Aren't you, darling?"

Nate glared at the dog, but Sarah could tell he was trying hard not to laugh. "Well, only one of us gets to sleep in bed with her, buddy, and that someone just happens to be me."

Sarah cringed. "Um, Nate, about that…"

He looked down at her and shook his head. "You're kidding me, right? We have to share your bed with the dog?"

Sarah laughed so hard she had tears streaming down her cheeks again. "'Fraid so."

Nate put her on her feet and took her hand. "When I proposed I had no idea what I signed up for, did I?"

She slipped her hand from his and pressed

her palms against his cheeks instead. "I do love you, Nate."

"Yeah," he said, glancing at the dog. "Me *and him.*"

Sarah dragged him by the hand up the porch steps and through her front door. "I have two men in my life. You're just gonna have to get used to sharing me."

But only Nate would ever make her feel the way she did right now. Loved for who she was.

Nate pulled the door shut behind them before backing her up against the wall, pinning her hands above her head and pushing his body against hers. "I don't share," he whispered, "especially when it comes to you."

Sarah couldn't stop laughing as he nibbled at her ear, then kissed her collarbone, before tracing a path back to her mouth.

"Are we clear about that?" he asked, his eyes shining.

"Oh, we're clear all right," she affirmed, wriggling her body closer to his. "It's just you and me, soldier."

"Damn right," he murmured in her ear. "I'm not ever letting you out of my sight again."

Sarah tilted her head back and shut her eyes. This was…bliss. And she didn't *ever* want Nate to stop.

* * * * *

Mills & Boon® Large Print
May 2013

BEHOLDEN TO THE THRONE
Carol Marinelli

THE PETRELLI HEIR
Kim Lawrence

HER LITTLE WHITE LIE
Maisey Yates

HER SHAMEFUL SECRET
Susanna Carr

THE INCORRIGIBLE PLAYBOY
Emma Darcy

NO LONGER FORBIDDEN?
Dani Collins

THE ENIGMATIC GREEK
Catherine George

THE HEIR'S PROPOSAL
Raye Morgan

THE SOLDIER'S SWEETHEART
Soraya Lane

THE BILLIONAIRE'S FAIR LADY
Barbara Wallace

A BRIDE FOR THE MAVERICK MILLIONAIRE
Marion Lennox

Mills & Boon® Large Print

June 2013

SOLD TO THE ENEMY
Sarah Morgan

UNCOVERING THE SILVERI SECRET
Melanie Milburne

BARTERING HER INNOCENCE
Trish Morey

DEALING HER FINAL CARD
Jennie Lucas

IN THE HEAT OF THE SPOTLIGHT
Kate Hewitt

NO MORE SWEET SURRENDER
Caitlin Crews

PRIDE AFTER HER FALL
Lucy Ellis

HER ROCKY MOUNTAIN PROTECTOR
Patricia Thayer

THE BILLIONAIRE'S BABY SOS
Susan Meier

BABY OUT OF THE BLUE
Rebecca Winters

BALLROOM TO BRIDE AND GROOM
Kate Hardy

0513 Rom LP